MEETINGS AT MIDNIGHT

TAMARA WHITLOW

For Charo Saunders
My best friend, my sister, my peace

FOREWORD

This book contains:
>   Scene containing SA
>   Coarse language
>   Drinking/drunkeness
>   Interracial couples
>   Secrets pertaining pregnancy
>   Arson

CHAPTER 1

GREG

"*T*axi!"

Her foot stomps on the ground in frustration as I watch yet another cab pass her by.

"Fucking great. I swear I hate this city."

Her voice caught my attention as I stepped out the bank. As I watched her hand waving, I couldn't help but notice her beautiful shape. I could only see her back until she turned sideways after the cab passed her by. I had briefly seen her profile through the clouded window in the bank with the loan officer. Her exaggerated 'thank you' as she walked out of the loan office made me smile. From where I sat, I couldn't see when she had walked out. The only sound was her scuffled footsteps towards the front door. Her voice intrigued me so I hurried my meeting along so that I could try and catch her outside. I quickly shake the bank managers hand as he stood with me at the door as I was leaving. I smiled my thanks to him and walked over to the curb where she was aggravatingly, mumbling to herself.

"Mind if I try?" I ask her.

Her face is turned up in exasperation as she looks at me. When our eyes connect, her face softens a little and she tries to

I

smile. Her brown eyes searched mine for a moment as if she was looking for something in particular.

She shrugs one shoulder and pushes a wayward curl from her face. "Sure. Good luck."

She pulls the strap of her large bag up onto her shoulder and steps back as I walk in front of her. I place two fingers under my tongue and whistle loudly. A taxi puts on its break lights and backs up a little to where we are standing. The woman's lip curls up and she rolls her eyes.

"Figures." She huffs.

I chuckle as she breaks a smile and shakes her head. I reach out and open the car door for her and she looks at me with an arched brow.

"Thank you."

Her voice is rich with a husky undertone. She's wearing no makeup and her dark brown skin looks smooth. As the door to the taxi closes, I break out of my thoughts and step back as the car drives away. I can see her turn around in the back seat to look at me and I curse myself for not getting her name. My phone buzzes in my pocket and I silence it as I watch the cab turn the corner.

Shaking my head, I look at the phone and groan. The meeting that was scheduled for later has been moved up a couple of hours. Breathing deeply, I walk towards my car so I can head back to the office. The bank manager comes running back out of the building looking around. Seeing as though I just had a meeting with him, I thought he was looking for me.

"Mr. Stapleton? Are you looking for me?"

He clears his throat and shakes his head. "N-No Mr. Devereux." He holds up a drivers' license. "A lady was in here a little bit ago with one of my loan officers and forgot her ID."

The picture on the front made me smile. "I know her."

He looks at me confused. "You do?"

I smile and nod my head. "I just put her into a cab and am going to see her later. I can take it to her."

He looked at me apprehensively. "What? It doesn't look like I would know her?"

His face turns red and he starts to trip over his words.

"N-No, sir."

"No? Is it because I'm clearly older than her?"

He really started to stumble over his words. "I didn't mean to imply that, sir."

I held my hand out and he stumbled again.

"I really shouldn't. I could get into a lot of trouble."

"No, you wouldn't. I'll make sure that I give it to her straight away, no worries."

He looked around and let out a long breath and reluctantly placed the ID in my palm. I nod my thanks and walk to my car.

"Don't look so down Stapleton, I just saved you the trouble of mailing it. I'll make sure to tell her what a great man you are."

His eyes blinked rapidly as I got into my car. I can tell he's already regretting handing me the ID. I give a wave as I pull away from the curb before he could change his mind and head to the address on the card. I smile down at her picture. *Nice to meet you, Veronica Mason.* The smile I felt cross my face shouldn't be that wide. I had to see her one more time. There is no way that I could only look into those brown eyes only once.

CHAPTER 2

VERONICA

"*J*ust need to see some ID please."

I start to search through my wallet and I can feel my heart start to race.

Fuck, fuck, fuck… Where is my ID? I close my eyes and grumble. *I left it at the bank.* I put a smile on my face and shake my head.

"I left my ID at the bank. You can just put it back."

The older man behind the register looked around and gave me a wink before pressing in some numbers.

"That'll be $29.37."

I let out a grateful sigh and gave him forty dollars. I usually get carded everywhere I go because of how young I look. I'm twenty-five but I don't look it.

"Thank you so much."

"No problem. Looks like you need a drink and who am I to get in the way of that."

I take my change and grab my bags. "Yeah, it's been a day."

He winked again with a chuckle, as I walked away from the counter and out the door. My apartment was only a block away and I just wanted to get my shopping done before I went home. After the fiasco at the bank this afternoon, I didn't want to go anywhere else. The heat felt good on my face as I walked in the sun. It had been cool the last couple of days so it felt amazing to feel the sunlight with no wind attached to it. There were a couple of kids playing curb ball as I passed by and I smiled at the idea of being that carefree again. I walked up the couple of stairs in front of my building and into the foyer. My apartment was on the first floor and I was grateful to not have to walk up flights of stairs. I let myself in and took in the fresh paint smell as I closed the door behind me. I looked at all of my paintings that lined the floor in the living room as I took my food to the kitchen and tried not to think about being rejected for yet another loan from the bank. I currently work in a warehouse packing office supplies but painting has always been my passion. I've been trying for years to get my work in front of the right crowd. If I could paint all day and make a living, I would. Not wanting to get myself down, I put my food up and started to prepare my chicken to put into the oven. As I washed my chicken in the sink, the doorbell rang and I could feel my brow furrow. *I'm not expecting anyone.* I quickly dried my hands and hurried to the door and looked out the peephole. Whoever it was, they had their head down so I couldn't see their face. When I swung the door open, I gasped. The man from the bank was standing at my door and I could feel my nerves getting the better of me. *His suit looked too expensive for this side of town. Not only that, but how did he find me?*

"Can I help you?"

I look out into the hallway to see if anyone else was out there. He was alone and when my eyes locked with his, he smiled and his smile was beautiful. His white teeth accentuated his tanned skin. He had green speckles throughout his hazel eyes, and the slight grey in his hair by his ears told that he was older even though the clean cut of his face didn't show it.

"You left this at the bank."

I looked down at his perfectly manicured hand and he held my ID. My eyes snapped back to his.

"They just gave this to you?"

He chuckled and held it out towards me and I took it from his grasp.

"No. I may have told them that I knew you."

"And again, they just gave it to you?"

He shrugged like it was nothing. "I guess I looked friendly enough."

"Yeah, so did every serial killer. Why would you go out of your way to bring this here? Looks like I need to have a nice talk with the bank."

"No, please. It's not their fault. I made them believe that I knew you. They really didn't want to give it to me."

"Nonetheless, they did. You still haven't told me why you brought this to me."

His head tilted to the side as he looked me up and down. My eyebrow was raised and my arms crossed by the time he looked back at my face.

I guess I have my answer. "Take in enough?"

His tongue ran across his teeth as his feet shuffled a little and I placed a hand on my hip.

"Maybe." *The nerve of this guy.*

His eyes looked over my shoulder and he looked back at me surprised.

"You're an artist?"

What the hell. First, he undresses me with his eyes and then his conversation shifts. "Trying to be."

"You mind if I see your work?"

I thrust my hand out in front of him as he started forward. He stopped short and look at my extended hand. With his expensive suit and cocky attitude, I could tell he isn't used to being told no.

"Hi. I'm Veronica and you are?"

His face softened and he looked reproved. His throat

cleared and he stood up a little straighter before placing his hand in mine. His slight smirk like he was surprised that I asked had my hackles up.

"I'm sorry. I'm Greg." He finally said.

He shook my hand and I opened the door enough for him to come in, still watching him like a hawk. He walked towards one of my favorite pieces and squat down to look closer at it. The painting was just of a shadowed profile of a woman with a multi-colored scarf wrapped around the outside of her hair with her large afro puff sat on top of her head. The lips were red and her eyes were closed. It was simple and I loved it because it reminded me of myself.

"How much for this one?"

I didn't think, I just spat out a number. "$2700."

"Will you take a check?"

What in the actual fuck? I threw that number out as a joke.

"Wait…What?"

He stood up tall from where he squats and looked at me. It was then I realized how tall he actually was. With us standing so close, my head stared at his chest. I took a step back because I didn't know this man and it wouldn't take much for him to take advantage of the situation. His words brought my eyes back to his face.

"A check? Will you take one?"

"Um, yeah."

He reached inside his jacket pocket and retrieved a checkbook.

"Who do I make it out to? Do you have a business name or something?"

"No. I just sell under my name. Veronica Mason."

"Do you have a license to sell these?" He asked as he scribbled across the checkbook.

I looked at him confused. "What if I say no, will you still buy it?"

"Of course, I will, but you know that you need a license to sell in New York."

"Those cost money and I'll get it when I can."

He gives me a short nod and finishes writing the check out. After he rips it from its sleeve, he hands it to me and picks up the painting. He's staring at it as he walks towards the door.

"Thank you for this." He stops at the door and looks over at where I still stood. "You know, she looks like you."

I can feel my face heat up. "Yeah. I know."

The smile he gives has meaning behind it but I didn't have time to figure it out as he opens the door and walks out. I run to the front window and watch as he gets into a silver Mercedes. *Boy, you'd better be glad that your car was still there.* This neighborhood isn't known for having a lot of white people in it. Especially ones that drive nice cars. As he pulls away from the curb, I look down at the check in my hand and inhale sharply. *$5000.* The note at the bottom says *good luck with your paintings and getting your license.* I look at the top of the check and have to hold onto the windowsill. *Gregory Devereux.* You would not be a New Yorker without knowing that name. He owned buildings all over the city. His face is on just about every billboard and now I feel stupid because I didn't recognize him standing right in front of me. He was one of the leading real estate gurus in the business and he just bought one of my paintings. *Holy hell.*

CHAPTER 3

VERONICA

"*I* sold a mother-fucking painting!"

A light chuckle sounded on the other end of the phone.

"Well, hello to you too Ronnie."

"Chantel, did you hear what I said?"

"Ronnie, everyone can hear you. Where did you sell it and how did the bank go?"

I could hear her fingers going across the keyboard as she typed. She worked from home in medical billing so she was always available for my ramblings. We've been best friends since the third grade and I always tell her that she would be my one phone call if I ever got arrested.

"The bank denied me again but I sold my painting here, at home."

The typing stopped and I heard the phone shuffle.

"How?"

"I left my ID at the bank and someone brought it to me."

"That's nice that the bank would do that."

"Actually, it was a man and he doesn't work there."

"WHAT! Ronnie! You can't just be inviting strange men into your apartment."

"It was Gregory Devereux."

The line was quiet for so long that I thought she hung up.

"Excuse me? Like, Devereux that owns like half the city?"

"Yep, and he bought a painting for $5000!"

"Shut the hell up, you're lying! Did he give you his number? Did he ask you out?"

I couldn't help but laugh. "No, why would he ask me out? He just brought me my ID."

"Because you're fine as hell, Ronnie. I think the biggest question is, why did he bring your ID to you?"

"I don't know. I didn't know who he was when I was at the bank. He helped me to get a cab and I was so angry about the loan that I didn't process who he was."

"Girl, no white millionaire will just show up to your house without a reason. He wants you."

I barked out a laugh. "Shut up! He was just being nice."

"No. Getting a cab is nice. Opening a door is nice. Driving across the city to hand deliver a drivers license is something else."

"Well, I didn't talk to him long and I didn't get his number so."

"Girl… I need more details. What did he smell like? He just looks like he smells like money. Is he as cute as he is in his pictures?"

"Chantel, that man smells divine." I curl my feet underneath my butt while I plop down on the couch. "His smile should be a work of art. I swear, I could listen to him talk for hours. His voice almost made my panties fall, it was so deep and quiet. I felt like I had to lean in closer to hear him fully."

"Girl, my panties would have evaporated."

We both start laughing and then I get serious.

"You don't know how badly I needed that sale. I can pay my rent and get the license I need to start selling legally. For a day that started off so horrible, it has shaped up to be one of the best days of my life."

"I'll bet and I do know. I wish I could have seen your face when you realized who he was."

"That's just it… I didn't know until I looked at his name on the check."

"Stupid girl! Sheesh. Hopefully he remembers you if you ever cross paths again."

"Yeah. Like that will ever happen. I'm just another black girl in the city to a rich man like that."

"You never know girl, you never know."

CHAPTER 4

GREG

"Mr. Devereux? Is there anything else you want to add?"

My eyes shoot up to the woman in the front of the room. Clearing my throat, I sit up straighter in my chair. We've been at this conference for the last two hours and I haven't heard a single word.

"Um, no. I think we're good."

The woman smiles and looks around the room at the other faces. Satisfied, she closes her folders and starts to pack up. Everyone starts to stand up and begin conversations and I shake my head.

"Hey." I look over to my partner who stands up with me. "Who is she?"

Not looking at him, I pick up my papers and stuff them in my briefcase.

"Who is who?"

I can feel his smile behind me and when I turn around, his face is gleaming.

"There has to be a girl. I haven't seen a look like that since Jennifer."

"Please don't mention her name. Every time you do, she calls and I've had enough with police reports."

My phone chose that moment to ring and we both looked at each other. Me and Riley have been friends since high school. His family moved a couple doors down from us when we were both sophomores. Our parents became quick friends and we've been inseparable ever since. We both played basketball together in college and when I started my business, I brought him in as my accountant. He's been the one person that I know I can trust with anything and I couldn't see doing this without him.

I looked at the screen and relaxed my shoulders. "It's Deena."

He barked a laugh and clapped my shoulder before heading to the door. I smile and answer the phone.

"Hey Deena."

"How did the meeting go?" She asked hopeful.

"I couldn't even tell you. I don't remember a thing. What's up."

She chuckled and I could feel her chiding me through the phone. She was the mother of our operation. I had already gone through three secretaries before I found her. She was a grandmother who just needed to get out of the house and work part time and now, I don't know where I'd be without her. She runs my whole organization.

"Your six o'clock canceled so you can just go home after you leave there. I'll close up here."

"You're a life saver, Deena."

"I know, you can't live without me."

"It's true."

"So, who is she?"

"What? Who?"

She giggled. "You're unfocused so it has to be a woman. You haven't acted like that since…"

"Stop. Don't say her name. You're worse than Riley."

She laughed outright at that. "Okay. Go home and get some rest. I'll see you tomorrow."

"Thanks. Be careful going home."

"Will do."

After hanging up, I chuckle and shake my head and go in search of Riley. I shook hands with the other agents as I passed by and hurried to the lobby. Riley was leaned against the front desk talking to a beautiful brunette. I roll my eyes at him as he makes eye contact and I snort. The woman he's with lowers her lashes at me and I break smirk. As I go to walk out, he catches up with a shit eating grin on his face.

"She wants to go out with me."

"Of course, she does."

"Not everyone is a gold-digger, Greg."

"They are when they know you're my best friend."

"Whatever. Her voice was annoying anyway, I would probably just fuck her."

I give him a look and he just shrug it off.

"So, are you going to tell me who she is?"

"There isn't anything to tell. I met a woman; she's an artist and it won't go anywhere."

"Why not?"

"Because she didn't seem interested."

"Did she know who you were?"

"I have no idea. She didn't mention it though."

"That might be a good thing. You could screw her and leave her alone."

"You're a horrible man, Riley."

He had the nerve to look hurt as I continued to the car. We rode together and I'm going to drop him off and try to put this woman behind me.

～

CHAPTER 5

"*D*o you ever think you'll call him?"

Me and Chantel are out to eat at one of the restaurants we would normally never eat in. With the money that came from selling that painting, I've had wiggle room to try new things. I look up over my steak and turn my lips up as I chew.

"No. I didn't even write down the number from that check. That's real stalkerish."

She rolled her eyes and took a bite of her salad.

"I think it would have been sweet. He probably wanted you to call him."

"He gave me my ID and bought a painting, if he wanted me to call, he would have given me his number, and if he did, what would I say? Hello, you bought a painting, let's go out to eat."

Her shoulder lifts in a shrug and she arches a brow.

"Maybe."

I chuckle and go back to my fifty-dollar steak. The atmosphere in the restaurant wasn't as stuck up as I thought it would be. We never venture downtown because, one, it's expensive, and two, we are broke. I told her that if they gave a hint of looking down on us, we would leave. There are people dressed to the nines and some in jeans. I have on a pair of brown slacks with my white shirt, and my thick hair is hidden underneath my scarf. I have it styled with only a small portion of my hair sticking out of the front and the scarf is wrapped in a beautiful knot in the front. Chantel is in business suit and we both look like we fit right in. I thought we would be the only ones of color in the place but there were black faces scattered throughout. We had been there for about an hour and the service has been amazing. Our waiter was very attentive and the food was delectable.

"You think he'll come back for another painting?"

"Chantel, I don't want to think about him. It's bad enough that I didn't recognize him. I'm just going to be grateful that he helped me out of two ruts; the cab and my rent."

"Okay, I'll leave it alone but things like this just don't happen to people like us. What do you want to do after this?"

I look around and make a face. "I don't know what to do around here. I think the museum is around here somewhere."

"Ooh! I haven't been to the museum since I was little."

"Me neither."

The waiter walked by and I flagged him down.

"Yes, ma'am." He stops with a smile.

"How close is the museum from here?"

He turned and pointed to the front door.

"When you go out, make a right and it's two blocks ahead."

"Thank you."

He smiled a toothy grin and gave a sharp nod as he continued on with his job.

"Think you can walk two blocks in those heels?" I ask Chantel.

"Girl, I have my flats in my purse. Don't play with me."

We both laugh and finish our glass of wine while we wait for the check to come. The waiter walked over and clasped his hands together and my heart dropped. *What was happening. I didn't even try to pay with my card yet so it couldn't be that.*

"You ladies have a wonderful evening; it's been a pleasure to serve you tonight."

I looked over at Chantel confused and she shrugged.

"Thank you? We just need the check."

He shook his head and looked around like he was keeping a secret. "It's already taken care of, miss."

My eyes rounded and Chantel looked nervously around.

"I'm sorry. What was that?" I ask in a hushed tone.

"Mr. Devereux is with some clients and said that you were his guests also. He's paid for your meal."

My eyes searched the restaurant until they found his. He was seated in the corner with four other people. Everyone was talking around him and his eyes were on me. I lifted my glass in salute and his smile lit up the room. He grabbed his drink and lifted the glass back. Chantel had almost broken her neck to see what was going on behind her. When her eyes met mine, the smile was so big on her face and I know her cheeks hurt. Chantel can be loud sometimes when she's excited and I had to get us out of there before she made a scene. I quickly thanked the waiter and we gathered our things and walked towards the door. I turned one more time to see his face but he was already back into his conversations. My heart was hammering in my chest as I willed my knees to keep me upright. As soon as we stepped outside, Chantel grabbed me and squealed.

"Girl, he is so fine, and he wants you!"

I chuckle and shake my head. "No. He was just being nice."

"Here we go with this nice talk again. That man was staring the soul out of your body."

"He is way out of my league."

Chantel gave me a frustrated look and put her fists up to me.

"I just want to shake you sometimes. You're beautiful and any man would be lucky to have you. Especially one with money." She winked.

I laughed and put my arm through hers.

"C'mon. Let's go."

Chantel quickly changed her shoes and we took in the night air and walked to the museum.

CHAPTER 6
GREG

I didn't want to come to this meeting, but I'm glad that I did. My eyes were drawn to her as soon as I walked in. She and her friend were laughing at something and the way her smile showed all of her teeth made me smile and had my stomach in knots. She looked perfect. This time she had on a little lipstick and her full lips looked to be begging to be kissed. I tried to focus on the voices around me but she laughed at something and heads turned her way. She looked embarrassed and covered her mouth as she tried to hold in a laugh and I found myself chuckling with her. They had her and her friend seated in the center of the restaurant and I was captivated. When I paid for her meal and she searched me out, I was lost when her eyes found mine. I could see the way her eyelids lowered from where I sat. I didn't even try to hide the fact that I wanted her and I had hoped she could see it on my face. She lifted her glass and I retuned the gesture. When she stood up to leave, I wanted to go to her but someone at the table called my name to ask me a question and I had to try to rejoin the conversation, even though I had no idea what had been said. Her back was to me by the time I looked her way and I couldn't help but notice the sway of her hips as she walked out with her friend and wished that I could join her. Just that brief interaction got my brain in motion. I needed to see her again and I knew just how I could do it.

After dinner was over, I quickly bid my goodbyes and shook hands before hurrying to my car. It's been so long since I've been excited about anything but work. This woman has taken up residence in my head and I'm going to pursue her. I chuckle as I make the drive to the other side of town. My brain goes to Jennifer and how crazy she was and me hoping that Veronica isn't like that but I may in fact be the crazy one this time. *Who just drives to someone's house to return an ID just to see them?* No, I'm not crazy, I'm persistent. Jennifer on the other hand, she was certifiable. She put on a great front before I found out that she was a stalker and a thief.

I dated Jennifer about three years ago and things were amazing between us. I felt like she got me and could even see myself with her long term. I met her at one of the rubbing elbows parties and we hit it off right away. Jennifer was beautiful and loved to laugh. I could listen to her laugh all day long. She was shy at first and after a couple of dates, she opened up to me about her family and how they treated her. I felt bad for her and was proud that she fought her way out of her families grasp. No one should have to be made fun of or bullied, even by family. I constantly reassured her that she was safe with me and when we made love the first time, it was magical. The way her body moved over top of mine and the way she was in the moment with me at every turn. She trusted me with her secrets and her body and I was in love. I couldn't get enough of her. It wasn't until Riley brought to my attention that he had overheard her on the phone with someone whispering about me. He overheard her telling someone that she would have money at the end of the week and that she had me right where she wanted me. I have a reputation and a business to protect and I confronted her about it. She of course, denied all of it but wouldn't make eye contact. We started fighting a lot and this was new. We had never raised our voices at each other and I couldn't understand what was happening. I hired someone to look into her past because some of her answers about her family began to change and I had to know what I was dealing with. Turns out, she hadn't fell out with her family. They actually had a great relationship. I flew to South Carolina and spoke with her mother, who hadn't seen her daughter in a couple of years. They had exchanged letters and text messages, but she hadn't talked to Jennifer in person, in some time. She didn't live in the house that I had been picking her up from either. The house belonged to a friend of hers. Everything that I had known about her was a lie. Those weren't deal breakers though because she could have a good reason for lying about it. It was when she stole some of my watches and a ring when she had spent the night that was the last straw. My name is engraved in all of my things and when the pawn shop called me, we watched the tapes and there she was, pawning my things. After I broke it off with her, she would show up to meetings, the gym, dinner, and just about anywhere I would end up. She would make a scene and I would have to call for security. My phone would ring at all hours of the night and I was exhausted. I had to get a restraining order against her. Just going through the struggle of getting rid of her turned me off from dating anyone at all. Hotels and sex were all I had time for. I vowed that there would be no one in my space again… Until now.

Snapping out of my thoughts, I pulled up to Veronica's apartment and saw that the lights were still out. Grabbing a piece of paper, I quickly wrote a note.

> *I really want to see you again and would love if you'd meet me*
> *tonight, at midnight at this address.*
> *G. Devereux*

Being in real estate, I had just about any and everything in my car, so I grabbed a piece of tape and hurried to place it on her door. Looking at my watch, it was nine-thirty and hurried back to my car. The address that I left her was one of my favorite spots to think. I owned the building and from the rooftop, you could see the lights of the city and just about every star in the sky. *Now, I just cross my fingers and wait.*

CHAPTER 7

VERONICA

I hugged Chantel before I got into my cab and started my way home. Tonight, was fun and I wish it didn't have to end. She had to go to work tomorrow so she couldn't stay out late. Me on the other hand, didn't have to be at work until one in the afternoon and I was wired. The cab jerked yet again as the traffic stopped. *This is the reason I don't drive downtown.* I have a car but it's easier to just use the subway or take a cab but at this time of night, the subway isn't safe. When I must drive downtown, there's never any parking and the streets are always packed. I only drive to work and back home because the idea of standing after work waiting for a ride was unappealing. We finally make it out of the heavy traffic and I scroll my phone as the driver makes his way down the narrow side streets. I glance out the window and take in how beautiful the city looks at night. The sky is lit up in colors from the billboards and bright neon lights of the different shops. All too soon, the darkness engulfs the cab as we leave the busy streets of the city. The music playing in the front was an upbeat afropop song and I could feel myself swaying to the beat as I perused my phone. As the cab came up to my apartment, I started to gather my things and I hand the driver a tip and hurried out. The street was quiet and it looked abandoned. There was usually at least one person outside or someone walking a dog, but tonight, there was no one. My footsteps were the only sounds as I hurried up the stairs. I saw the paper taped to the door as soon as I opened the outside door. I cursed as I thought it was a letter from the landlord. My heart skipped a beat as I stood in the hallway and read the words. My eyes darted this way and that as though he could be hiding in the corner somewhere. Unlocking my door, I quickly threw my purse on the counter and read the note again. It felt like I was going to throw up with the anxiousness coursing through my body. *He wants to see me. Maybe Chantel was right.* The paper in my hands started to shake and I looked at my hands. I placed the paper on the counter because I couldn't see the words anymore. *What should I do?* It was eleven o'clock and I didn't have long to figure it out. If I called Chantel, she would talk my ear off and then I'd be even more nervous. For the first time in my life, I didn't think, I just grabbed my keys and my purse and left back out the door.

CHAPTER 8

GREG

I'm not sure she's even going to show. After I left her apartment, I spent the last couple of hours setting up a table, some candles, a bottle of wine and some flowers on the rooftop of my building. I'm standing here watching the lights from the cars below pass by and hope that one of them might stop. I don't know why I want to see this woman again. It's not like we had some meaning conversation and hit it off, I barely even talked to her. I have her painting set up in my office and Deena looked at me like I was crazy when I told her where I had gotten it. Me, being a white man with this bold painting of a beautiful black woman on my wall with no kind of backstory confounded her. She was engrossed in my story and when I was through she encouraged me to talk to her, so here I am. I glanced down at my watch and it was a quarter till twelve and I sighed. *I probably scared her away. That was bold of me to put that note on her door. I should have just waited until tomorrow and asked her out for real. I'm so stupid to think that she would just drop every-thing and come here. What if she has a man and he gets there first.* Now I'm panicked and turn around to hurry to retrieve the note. I'm stopped in my tracks as she's standing right there. The smirk on her face is cute as her eyebrows narrow.

"Everything okay? You look worried."

I cleared my throat and squared my shoulders.

"Um, no. I'm fine. How are you?"

Her head tilts to the side as she takes in the table. Her chin lifts.

"What's all this?"

I turn around and look. "A little wine and some snacks."

She's looking at me like she's trying to figure something out.

"I see that but what's all this for?"

I smile and wave a hand in invitation to her to sit down and she cautiously makes her way over.

"I just thought that I would try to get to know you a little."

"At midnight?"

"Why not?"

My answer must have been right because she made a face of approval and sat down in the chair that I pulled out for her.

"It's beautiful up here. Is this your building?"

I looked out at the twinkling lights and the stars and nodded.

"Yeah. This was the very first building that I bought. There is nothing here, it's just a building and I love to come here and think. Wine?"

She nodded and I uncorked the bottle and poured us a glass. We clinked glasses and took a sip. Her eyes closed in appreciation.

"This is good."

"It's one of my favorites."

She places the glass on the table and I can see her shiver a little. Being this high, the breeze that comes across is cold. I quickly take my jacket off and place it over her shoulders. She smiles her thanks as I take the seat across from her. Her eyes are looking up at the stars in amazement.

"The stars look so close up here."

"Yeah, I love it here."

When she looks back at me, I get butterflies. Her eyes seem to take everything in.

"So…"

I cleared my throat and shuffled in my seat. I hadn't been this nervous since I graduated college and had my first real interview.

"I have no idea what I'm doing. I saw you and for some reason, I can't get you out of my head."

"Why? Did I do something special?"

I shake my head. "That's just it. You didn't do anything at all. It's something about you that makes me want to know more."

"There's nothing to tell. I work in a warehouse on the southside. My parents are still married and live in Philly. I love to paint and that's about it. I'm nothing special at all."

She has no idea how beautiful her soul is. It's like I can see her heart in her eyes. I'm so enamored by her.

"I have your painting in my office."

"Really? That's awesome."

"Yeah. It feels like I can see you when I look at her."

"That's not creepy."

I couldn't help but laugh and her smile lit up her face. I took my phone and opened the music app. A slow song started to play and I stood up and put my hand out. She took it and I pulled her to stand. She looks beautiful in her brown pants and white flowing shirt. The wind is blowing lightly and the shirt hugs her curves and shows off the form that she's trying to hide. Pulling the jacket from her shoulders, I drape it on the chair. I took one of her hands and the other went to my chest and her perfume had me closing my eyes to take it in. I placed my hands on the small of her back and pulled her close. She let me lead as we swayed to the beat. Cars honked in the distance and the occasional sounds of someone yelling could be heard but for a moment, it was just the two of us.

"I don't know what it is about you, but this can't be the last time that I see you."

"Then it won't be the last time."

With those words, I gripped her tighter and let out the breath that I was holding. It felt to good to let her go.

CHAPTER 9
VERONICA

When I walked into the building, everything was dark. There was a line of lights on the floor that lead to an elevator. A sign was handwritten that read 'top floor.' My hands were sweating and I could feel my body shaking as I pressed the button and rode the elevator up to the top floor. I questioned myself all the way over here and now that I'm here, I'm scared to death. When the elevator dinged, I stepped off to another paper taped to the wall with an arrow pointing down the hallway. This hallway was completely lit and I followed it to a door at the end. I pushed the door open and the night air breezed past my face. I peeked out and at first, I didn't see anyone but as I stepped out, I seen him standing there looking over the side of the building. He was wearing a dark suit and his hands were in his pockets. His hair blew gently in the wind. He looked to be deep in thought and didn't turn around as I approached. I froze when he suddenly turned and started for me. His face looked haunted and he froze when he saw me. I wasn't sure if he was having second thoughts or not. We stood there and stared for a minute before any words were exchanged. I was going to leave but something told me to stay and I'm glad I did. We both relaxed as our conversations continued. As we danced, his arms felt good around me and his heartbeat was comforting as I rested my head on his chest.

"I don't know what it is about you, but this can't be the last time that I see you."

"Then it won't be the last time."

Where did that confidence come from? I could feel his body relax at my words and the mood was lighter. It was like he was ready for me to say no. This felt way too good to say no to. We danced for another song before we sat back down and ate the cheeses and fruit he had on a tray. It was two-thirty in the morning before I started to yawn. We had talked and laughed and something about tonight had me wanting more.

"I'm sorry for keeping you out this late. I'm so glad you came."

"Me too. I had a good time tonight."

"As did I. Can we meet here again this weekend?"

I smiled and looked up into his handsome face. "Yeah, I'd like that. How about Saturday…at midnight."

He barked a laugh and nodded. "It's a date."

He walked me out and to my car and was the perfect gentleman. I was nervous that he would try to kiss me but he just opened my car door and allowed me to slip inside. He waved as I backed out of the parking spot and my ride home was on auto pilot. I thought about how adorable his laugh was and how his eyes had lines that crinkled every time he smiled. The feel of his light stubble tickling my forehead as we danced. I wanted to feel his lips on mine and that thought scared me a little. Every time he licked his lips, I could imagine them on mine. He was walking perfection. I slept so well while I dreamed of his body on top of mine.

∼

"Earth to Ronnie!"

I snapped out of my thoughts as I noticed how many boxes, I had missed go past me.

"I'm sorry. I had a long night and I'm not feeling too well."

My manager shakes his head and looks down at his clipboard.

"Look, why don't you just go home and get some rest. We are just about done here anyhow."

"Thank you. My brain isn't working to good today."

"Well, try to get it together by tomorrow. We have a huge order to fill."

"Yes, sir."

I hurried my apron off and headed to my locker to put my things away. As I shut my locker, I looked at my phone and laughed. I don't even remember texting Chantel when I got home but she had responded to my text.

You had better call me as soon as you get off!

I looked at what I had sent her and groaned.

I just left Devereux.

No wonder she's freaking out. I'll call her when I get home. I'm not ready to share him yet.

CHAPTER 10

GREG

"Spill. You've been smiling for weeks now and I want to know why."

Riley bites into the apple he's holding and plops down on the couch in my office. He puts his feet up on the table in front of him and watches me closely. The pen in my hand twirls between my fingers as I stare at the painting on the wall.

"It's the painter, isn't it?"

I smile and place the pen down on the desk. I steeple my fingers under my chin and smile.

"Yeah. I've seen her a couple times already and she's perfect."

Riley's feet hit the floor and he sat up straight. He wipes the juice from the apple from his chin as he waits for me to finish.

"Remember I told you that I had paid for her dinner?" He nods. "Well, I wrote her a note to meet me at my building across from the park at midnight. I didn't think she would come, but she did. We talked and danced and talked some more. Her words are like poetry. Everything that comes out of her mouth is like a song. Not only is she beautiful, but she's smart as hell and as you can see, super talented."

"Have you slept with her yet?"

I picked up the pen and threw it at him and he ducked out of the way.

"You're such a pig."

"This coming from the man that screwed that waitress a month ago in the bathroom."

I rolled my eyes. "I can't treat her like that."

"Why not? And don't tell me it's because she's black?"

"Riley! Race has nothing to do with this."

"What? I'm serious. You've never dated a black woman before and she sounds like she's too good for you anyway. I should talk to her."

"You will stay the hell away from her."

Riley smiled mischievously. "You do like her. Damn. When can I meet her?"

"I'm not sure I want you to but, we're meeting again tomorrow."

"I'm happy for you. You deserve a little bit of happiness after you know who. You've got to keep me in the loop."

"Yeah, we'll see."

I watch him leave out of my office and try to get back to work but my mind was constantly on her. We talked about everything and nothing at all. One of our meetings on the rooftop consisted of just looking at the stars because she's never just taken a moment to look up at the stars. Another time, we talked about our parents and how we aimed to make them proud of us. I lost my parents early in my teenage years and grew up with different family members so, it was amazing to listen to her telling me about growing up in such a loving home with both parents. It was like each time we text and asked to meet, we were hiding from the world. I don't have to be someone else; I feel comfortable with her and that's rare. I have never felt so connected to someone as much I did Veronica. To have kept these meetings from Riley, my best friend, lets me know that I needed this just as much as she says that she needed it.

CHAPTER 11

VERONICA

"**W**hen am I going to get to meet him?"

I stir the pot on the stove while Chantel sits at the small island and stares me down.

"I don't know. These secret dates have been so nice. It's like we are hiding from the world and I get to see a side of him that people don't know."

"This is like a movie. I wonder what's going to happen when you show up to a function on his arm."

"Yeah, no. I'm not going to be that girl."

"What girl? You don't think he wants to show you off?"

I shake my head. "No. I'm just a regular ole girl and he's rich. I am not trying to be labeled a gold digger."

"But y'all haven't even slept together yet."

My mind went back to the last date that we had. I wore a pair of leggings and a long button up shirt that came past my thighs. As we danced on top of the roof, his hands slowly rubbed my hips and my butt. I had braided my hair into a crown around my head and adorned it with gold clips and he was mesmerized. His hands moved their way up my body and to my neck where his fingers lightly glided up under my braid. He tilted my head up and when his lips descended to mine, I couldn't help but to moan. This caused him to deepen this kiss and when his tongue snuck past my lips, I had to break away because I was ready to give him anything he wanted. We were both breathing hard and I had to squeeze my thighs together and bite my lip before I did something I wasn't ready for. He took my hand and pulled me to him and pecked my lips again before holding my hand while we danced again. It was perfect.

"Ronnie!"

My eyes snapped over to her and then down to the water boiling over in the pot.

"Shit. I'm sorry."

"Girl, you've got it bad."

I turned the heat down on the pot and let out a breath.

"I really like him but I feel like I'm setting myself up for a huge letdown."

"It'll all work out."

"I hope so. I just don't need complications right now. I finally have someone interested in allowing me to join their art show and I need to focus."

"That is so cool. When is the show?"

"In a month. I'm so nervous. If I can manage to sell some of these pieces, I can finally quit that damn job."

"I think you'll sell out."

"You have to say that because you're my best friend."

"Whatever. I love your work and I think you don't charge enough for them."

"Until I get my name out there, I have to think about selling just one."

Chantel sniffs the air. "Hurry up, I'm hungry."

I laugh and shake my head and finish dinner.

～

CHAPTER 12

GREG

"No! That is not the price that we agreed on. If you can't honor our agreement, I'll have my clients go elsewhere."

The door to the office cracks open and Deena pokes her head in. I wave her in and go back to my phone call.

"Well, when you figure out where those numbers came from then call me back. You have until the end of the day."

I hung up the phone and growled as I pulled my hair.

"I swear, that man is going to drive me to drink."

Deena chuckled and handed me a file.

"What's this?"

She points to my hand. "That is a new building on the upper east side. Just came on the market and the seller wants it sold right away. He called just a little while ago to see if you could take it on and of course, I told him you could."

I look at the pictures and whistle.

"Why would they want to sell this? It's beautiful."

She shrugged. "Not my business. I just take phone calls."

I chuckled at her. "Yeah, and so much more." She smiled and started for the door. "Thanks. I'll go and take a look."

She gave a short nod and stopped abruptly. "Please don't buy it for yourself."

I chuckled and nodded as she continued out the door. She knows me too well. If I see something I like, I'll scoop it up and sell it for more. I salute her and she laughs as she closes the door. This building stands alone and has windows from floor to ceiling all the way around. It's rare to find stand alone buildings anywhere in New York so this will go fast. There was no time to waste so I grab my keys and hurry out the door.

The building was more than what the pictures showed. The inside was empty but it would make an excellent storefront or even an office building. I called the owner and he wanted to sell it for three hundred thousand. That wasn't a bad price, especially for a standalone, and I hurried on the phone with some clients that were looking for a retail space. One of my long-time clients had been looking for a place for his granddaughter who was starting out in retail and I sent him pictures. He was all in and by the end of the day, the place was sold for three hundred and fifty thousand dollars. This is what I do, this is how I make my life work. People know me as the person to buy or sell your properties quick. It's only been a couple of hours and I'm set to already make one hundred thousand and ninety dollars. That is, if everything goes as planned, Deena would be pissed if she found out what I just did. My services aren't cheap and my commission is priced high for the jobs that I do. I wanted to celebrate and I knew that Riley was out of town for the day and I had no one to call. I would love to see Veronica but she's already said that she loved our late-night rendezvous and wasn't ready to go out. Guess I'm alone tonight. I stopped by the store and grabbed a bottle of Jack Daniels and headed home. I had no meetings on the books and if Deena needed me, she knew where to find me.

$\sim$

This would be the last time that I fell asleep drunk with a woman on my mind. I tossed and turned as I dreamt about brown skin on top of mine. Loose curls flowing through my fingers and body heat up under me. I woke up drenched in sweat. It was only five in the morning and I was hard as a rock. I got in the shower and tried to take care of things but I couldn't. Every time I closed my eyes, I saw her full lips and beautiful smile. I hurried clothes on and grabbed my keys. I couldn't take it anymore, I had to see her.

CHAPTER 13
VERONICA

I groaned as I heard the banging again. I looked at the clock beside my bed and it was only six-thirty. I lay there and hoped that they would just go away because there is nothing anyone could want this early in the morning. When the banging sounded again, I growled and threw my legs over the side of the bed. I put on my robe and padded barefoot to the door. I didn't even check the peephole. My sleep was priceless to me and if I'm woken up, I'm not in a good mood. I snatched the door open.

"What the hell do you want!?"

I sucked in a breath at the sight before me. Greg stood there with his hair disheveled and it looked like he hadn't slept in weeks. I pulled my robe tighter around me as I took in the sight of him.

"Greg, what's wrong? What are you doing here? Are you okay?"

His hazel eyes looked down at my lips and I felt my eyes round. He stepped forward and I took a step back. He still hadn't said anything and now I was getting worried.

"I can't do this anymore." He muttered.

There was a hint of alcohol on his breath and I looked at him confused.

"What?"

"This. I can't stay away from you. I think about you all day and all night. You're a constant thought in my head and I…"

"You what?"

His eyes closed like he was trying to center himself and when they opened back up, there was a hunger in his face that couldn't be denied. He closed the distance and grabbed the door and slammed it shut. My back bumped into the island and I gasped as he stood in front of me. My hair was all over my head and I only had on a pair of shorts and a tank top under my robe. His body cornered me against the island and I could see my chest heaving with each breath. His eyes never left mine until his hands went to the counter behind me and his head came down. The kiss was primal. He didn't take his time and ease me into it, it was raw. His hands went to my shoulders and slipped under my robe and he pushed it to the floor. His lips left mine but stayed close.

"Where's your bedroom?"

I had a choice. I could tell him to screw off or I could give in to the temptation that stood before me. I chose temptation.

"That way."

He stalked away from me and I followed in behind him. His shirt came off as he walked and by the time he was standing beside my bed, his sweatpants were low on his hips. His body turned to greet me as I walked up behind him and he took my face in his hands and whispered against my lips.

"I have no idea what you're doing to me but I'm lost."

As he kissed me, he raised my tank top and we parted so he could remove it. I didn't have on a bra so he had a front row seat to my breasts. He bent down and took one of my nipples into his mouth and I groaned at the suction. My hands went into his hair to keep him there just a little longer. He walked me backwards until my knees hit the bed. When he stood up, his eyes never left my chest. He placed his hands in the waist-band of his sweats and pushed them down. My eyes took in his body. With the suits that he wears and the way that his clothes fit him, you'd expect him to be sculpted but he was… normal. As we danced on the rooftop, I felt the slight roundness of his stomach but his suits always fit to a tee. There was no six pack, no hard pecks. He was beautiful. I showed him that I was ready by pushing my shorts to the floor and he smiled.

"You're so goddamned beautiful."

I didn't say anything as I sat on the bed and scoot myself back. I put my hand out in invitation and he quickly took it. He climbed up on the bed and his knee went into the junction of my thighs. I grazed my nails into his scalp and pulled him forward. Our lips met and his body lay on top of mine. I opened my legs to give him better access and he lined himself up with me and pressed forward. I moaned as he filled me and his head went to my shoulder as his body shuddered.

"Please don't move. I'm about to explode and I haven't even started."

I chuckle and my walls must have moved because he hissed. When he gained control of himself, he began to move. My hands gently scratched his back as he kissed my neck and my breasts. When he lifted my legs over his forearms, he started a rhythm that threw me over the edge. I cried out and the smile that crossed his face was adorable. His hands moved slowly over my body as he looked down where our bodies were joined. After I exploded yet again, his pace sped up and he threw back his head and groaned. He seated himself as far as he could inside me and I gasped. I could feel him jump inside of me as his body lay gently down over top of me. He didn't immedi-ately remove himself from me. He placed my legs back down and propped himself up above me.

"That was amazing."

I smiled and pushed the hair from his forehead. "It was."

He kissed me softly as he pulled out of me and then lay on the side of me. Before I knew it, his eyes were closed and his breathing deepened. I chuckled and curled into his side. It didn't take me long to fall back to sleep as I listened to him breathe. *What in the world did I just do?*

CHAPTER 14

VERONICA

*T*he sound of buzzing woke me up. I absently felt the nightstand for my phone and looked at it, but it wasn't my phone ringing. I lifted my head and pulled the sheet up over my breasts as I saw the sleeping figure next to me. This morning came crashing back to me. I could feel my nipples peak at the thought of his hands on my body. I look over to where his pants are sitting on the floor and see the pocket lit up from his phone. I quickly reach over and put my tank top on and then contemplate whether to wake him up. He was sleeping so well and his face was buried in the pillow. The phone stopped buzzing and then started up again. I looked at the time and it was ten thirty. I lightly rubbed his back.

"Greg."

He groaned and buried himself deeper in the pillow.

"Greg." I said a little more sternly. One of his eyes slightly opened and he smiled.

"Good morning."

I smiled back. "Good morning. Your phone is ringing."

He lifted his head and listened. "What time is it?"

"Ten thirty."

His head fell back to the bed and he closed his eyes with a grunt.

"Dammit."

"Do you want me to hand it to you?"

He gave me a mischievous look with a grin.

"What I want is for you to take that shirt back off and let me put us back to sleep."

I couldn't help but laugh. He was too cute.

"As much as I want to allow you to do that, I have to get ready for work this afternoon."

He closed his eyes and a little whine rose from the pillow he was buried into. "Fine. Yes, please hand me my phone."

I reached to the floor and pulled the phone from his pocket and handed it to him. He turned over and looked at the screen.

"Shit."

"Is something wrong?"

"I hope not. Hold on."

He pressed the number that was on the screen and even though it wasn't on speaker, I could still hear.

"Gregory Xavier Devereux. Where in the hell are you?"

"Deena, what's wrong?"

"You told Chapman that he had until last night to come with an offer and he's here in your office. I've been calling you for an hour!"

"I'm sorry. Can you please get my suit out of the closet in my office and put it in the bathroom? I'll be there as soon as I can."

"Yeah, yeah. You'd better be glad I love your ass because this man is a piece of work. I don't get paid enough for this shit."

When he laughed, his whole face lit up.

"I'll give you a nice bonus. I'll see you in a minute."

He hung up and sighed. He looked at me with regret.

"Can I make it up to you?" I nodded and he leaned over and kissed me. "Good. I'll call you later."

With that, he got out of bed and walked naked to the bathroom. The shower came on and I pulled my knees up to my chest. It wasn't long until I joined him in the shower and he knelt down on the floor and worshipped me with his mouth. I was boneless by the time he left my apartment. *This man is going to make it hard to stay away from him.*

CHAPTER 15

VERONICA

a *week. That's how long it's been since I've heard from Greg. I knew that I shouldn't have slept with him. He got what he wanted and now he's in the wind.* I've called but my calls have gone unanswered. My texts haven't been answered either. After the fourth day, I gave up. I wouldn't chase him. I'm sitting on the floor at Chantel's house in front of the couch while she works. I didn't want to be in that apartment alone. His cologne was still on my pillows even though I changed the sheets. I can't walk into the bathroom without thinking about how his mouth made me come twice in the shower. The more I think about how beautiful our night was and how he just disappeared... I couldn't just sit there.

"Hey. You want Chinese?"

I look up over the back of the couch where she's standing with the phone in her hand.

"Yeah. That sounds good."

Her smile is full of pity and she was ready to curse him out after I told her what happened. I literally had to stop her before she went to his office. Things like this happen all the time and why should I be exempt from it. I've always been so careful with whom I spend my time with and I should have known that deviating from what I know, would end up like this. I shouldn't have come over here but her house is the only one I feel comfortable at. I was going to go and surprise my parents but they were getting ready for a cruise and I didn't want to bring their excitement down. The fact that Greg so casually smiled and kissed me before he left has me almost in tears. *Did that night mean nothing to him? This is why the rich shouldn't mingle with the common folk. It doesn't mix well.* My thoughts cleared as I looked at the breaking news on the tv. There was a burned down building and the smoke was still billowing. The news lady was fighting her way through a crowd to get closer to the scene. She was speaking to an officer and it was then that I noticed behind her a familiar face. Greg stood there in his expensive suit with a smile on his face and his hand lay on the small of a woman's back. The woman stood close to him and his hand ran small comforting circles on her back. The intake of breath behind me told me that Chantel was standing there and she saw it too. I looked at her and her face began to blur. I hated crying and he was certainly not someone to cry over. So, we had a couple of dates. It's not like we were exclusive or anything. But seeing him there with another woman just hurt.

CHAPTER 16
GREG

*M*y head was killing me. It has been nonstop all week. I left Veronica's house that morning and I have been sleeping at my office for the last couple of nights. Chapman finally came through with the right price for his commercial business and my clients were ready to draw up the papers. As soon as we finalized their sell, the building that I had just sold to a client's granddaughter had been burned to the ground. My company is now trying to clear our name from having anything to do with it. My client that wanted this property had to wait until the following weekend to purchase it due to some financial issues. I knew that this property would sell fast so I did what any good real estate broker would do, I purchased it myself with the hope of selling it to him when his funds were available. Turns out, he didn't have time. The place was torched and now we are trying to figure out who did it and why. I'm now out of money with this property and the police think that it's an insurance scam. Deena and Riley, both read me the riot act because they didn't know what I had done until after the fire. My life turned upside down in a matter of days. I'm now standing out here in front of the news and a burned down building with my sister, who is also, my lawyer. It's chilly and the smoke stinks but I'm not going to hide in the shadows because I know I had nothing to do with this. This is what I do best, smile on the outside and am exhausted on the inside. I just need a couple of hours of sleep but I know that it's going to be impossible for a while.

Two weeks had passed and it's been nonstop meetings at the police station and paperwork. It turns out that the granddaughter of my client burned it to the ground because she was mad at her grandfather. We also found out that this isn't the first time she acted out against him when she was upset. She didn't want any gifts from him and didn't know that he hadn't purchased it yet. Her apology was half-hearted at best and I was simply over them both. Her grandfather ended up giving me my money back but the damage had already been done. The stress and anxiety that I've been through this past month has been horrible. Let alone, Deena and Riley trying to smooth things over. My business has suffered because some people didn't want to wait for the truth. They jumped ship and judged me guilty right away. Insurance fraud doesn't look good on your record. After I received my money from the sell, I remembered that I never explained things to Veronica. It's been all over the news so I was hoping she put two and two together. I visited her apartment a couple of times and she either hasn't been home or she's not answering the door. Her number has been changed and there is no way I could get ahold of her. I feel like I've lost my best friend and it's my fault. I left her without an explanation and I know she probably hates me. I've got to get my business back on track and hopefully I can find her in the meantime.

CHAPTER 17

*I*t's been a month since I've left my apartment. I moved in with Chantel and have been loving it. It's helped me to save money and her company has been much needed. I'm getting ready for another showing of my paintings and my nerves are getting the best of me. The first showing that I had a couple of weeks ago went so well, that I got invited to another one with a well-known local artist. The curator that's hosting the showing called and said that tickets have been sold out for weeks. This is the first time that I get to show the world my paintings with camera crews and all, and I'm excited. Chantel has helped me pick out the best ones and having her opinion is wonderful. The one's she picked were full of color and excitement, unlike mine that were dreary and sad. The show is tomorrow and tonight we are celebrating. We just dropped my pieces off at the venue and we will be surprised with everyone else to see the setup. Chantel took the roast that she was cooking out of the oven and sat it on the counter. I took my glass of wine and walked over to her. I took in a whiff of her food and smiled. The smile immediately faded and I ran to the trash can. My whole body hurt as my stomach emptied.

"Damn girl. You said you were nervous but I've never seen you this nervous." Chantel stated as she began to rub my back.

Still standing over the trash can, I smiled. "Yeah. It's been like this for two days now. I hope I'm not getting sick."

"Or pregnant."

I chuckled and then we froze and looked at one another.

"Fuck no." I exclaimed.

"No. You're not. It's just nerves."

I nodded rapidly. "Yep. Just nerves."

"I'm fucking pregnant."

I can't believe that I just said those words out loud. I told Chantel that I was going to grab some paper towels and ended up in the aisle that I never would have seen myself in and bought a test. I asked the cashier for the bathroom and her eyebrow raised in an accusatory way as she pointed to the back. I thanked her and asked to leave my paper towels at the counter while I used the restroom. My heart raced as I took the test and I stared as the lines came up so fast that I thought the test was broken. I took the other one with the same results. *What in the fuck.* I hurriedly washed my hands and smiled my thanks to the cashier as I grabbed my bags and hurried out of the store. The smirk on her face as I was leaving told a whole story. I was on autopilot as I drove back home. *What in the hell was I supposed to do? Do I call him? Do I keep it? Do I move away to never be seen again?* I'm at a loss. I hadn't been with anyone after Greg and I was scared. I never wanted this, and to be labeled something, other than an artist is something I'm not prepared for. So, for now, I'm not going to tell anyone yet. I'll figure this out after the show. *Fuck.*

CHAPTER 18

GREG

I've been in a horrible mood for the last month or so and Riley finally talked me into going out tonight. A friend of his is having an art exhibit and he thought it would be nice to get out of the house. I'm not much for black tie events right now, but I can't stay cooped up in the house all day. I grab my tux out of the garment bag in the closet and hang it up on the hook on the door. I sit on the side of the bed and groan. The more I stare at it, the more I'm not feeling it at all. The sigh that left me came from deep in my stomach. When I see any art, I immediately think of the one that got away and I don't want to try and process those feelings all night long. After battling internally for about a half hour, I made my decision. I'm not going. I grab my phone.

"Hey. I'm not going."

"Greg. Come on! You've been moping around for weeks now and I can't take it anymore."

"Riley, you have been privy to everything going on. As my accountant, you can see what this has done to me. I don't want to smile in the faces of everyone who gave me the side eye just a few days ago."

"Man. I just want to see you happy again."

"Thanks for looking out but maybe we can grab dinner this weekend."

"Alright. Damn bro. I was really looking forward to you coming with me."

"There will be other shows. Take some pictures if they allow it and send them to me."

"Okay. Call you later."

"Cool."

After I hang up, I feel the weight of being out in public lift off of me. I'm just not ready to be out there yet. My business has suffered tremendously and trying to figure out how to keep the lights on has been my main focus. I went from wealthy to maintaining in a matter of weeks. In my mental state, I'm not sure how I would react if someone mentioned something about what I was going through. I'm just not ready for the judgmental eyes of those who cast me aside so easily.

CHAPTER 19
VERONICA

Oh my god. My cheeks hurt from smiling so much. The place is packed and people are loving my work. I giggle at Chantel who has a man cornered. They have hit it off since the beginning and I know he hasn't looked at any art because, his eyes have been on Chantel the entire night. She had good taste though. He was a tall black man with long locs tied in the back of his head. His suit shined in the low light of the room. It had silver accents throughout that brought out the silver streaks in his hair. I turned my focus back to the room and had to close my eyes and reopen them a couple of times to see the masses of people fancying my art. The night was coming close to an end and a large man with balding hair came over to me and placed his hand out.

"Mrs. Mason, I presume."

"It's Miss, and yes, I'm her."

"My name is Tyler Cunningham and I own a couple of night clubs in Vegas and am a promoter. I love your work and wonder if you have a business card so that I could speak to you or your management about purchasing or showing some of your work."

"Absolutely." I reach into my small purse and am grateful

that I had purchased some business cards earlier this month. I hand one to him and he smiles.

"Thank you so much. I love everything here. It's so vibrant and alive. Exactly what we are looking for."

"I really appreciate that."

He nodded his thanks and returned to mingling with the crowd. By the time the night was over, I had sold all but one of my paintings and taken so many pictures, my eyes were still adjusting from the camera flashes to the dark of the night. I handed out almost all of my cards and when I looked at my phone, I had over twenty text messages from potential clients looking for original pieces. My brain couldn't comprehend how one show could change my life so quickly. I had enough money to put a down payment on a house if I wanted to and I couldn't wait to see it all add up in my bank account. Hopefully the bank doesn't put a freeze on my assets due to me making so much in one day. I hurried and gave the curator a hug and thanked him for inviting me. He immediately asked to keep in touch for the next showing. With the money that I've made today, I'm going to give my two weeks' notice at the warehouse and buy more supplies to paint. My dream of becoming a paid artist is finally coming to pass. *Who knew that I would find out I was pregnant and make more money than I've dreamed about all in the same week?*

I waited until the week died down to tell Chantel about the baby. Of course, she was upset that I hadn't told her and she wanted me to tell Greg but I couldn't. He made his choice when he didn't come back and after hearing all of those stories about what he's dealing with, I didn't want to add anything else on him. I felt bad when I walked past a couple and overheard a conversation about what happened at that burned down building. It doesn't take away the sting of seeing him with that other woman but I felt bad none the less. Nope, I will keep this between me and Chantel for the time being. I don't want to deal with baby drama at the beginning of what could be my career. If I tell the world that I'm pregnant and it plays out in the news, I could lose everything before I even touch it. My decision is made and hopefully she can live with that.

CHAPTER 20

GREG

The weekend is here and I'm kind of excited to get out of the house. I've been focusing on my mental health and hitting the gym a lot more. Me and Riley are going out to eat today and my stomach growls just from thinking about it. We're going to a local pub that's known for their great wings draft on tap. As I walk in, my nervousness dissipates as I see the crowd of people laughing and dancing. The atmosphere is just what I needed. Glasses clanked, bodies swayed to the beat of the music and no one looked our way. It was perfect. We found two seats at the bar and watched the crowd as we waited for the bartender.

After a while, we had a couple of beers and danced with a couple of women before we sat back down to order some food. Riley gave me his phone to show me pictures of the art exhibit as we waited for our food. It looked like everyone was having a great time. There were tons of people in the pictures and everyone was smiling or laughing. As I continued to scroll, I almost dropped the phone.

"She was there?" My heart was hammering in my chest as I looked at Riley for an answer.

His face was confused as he looked at the phone.

"Who? Oh, yeah. She was one of the featured artists. Super nice and beautiful too."

I was quiet as I stared at her smiling face. She looked so happy and all I could picture was her smiling face above mine as she looked down at me.

"Do you know her? I think her name is…"

"Veronica." I answered.

Now his attention is piqued and he still hadn't put two and two together. "Wait… How do you know her?"

"Remember when I met a woman and we met on roof of my building?"

His eyes grew large. "THAT was her?"

I could only nod as I looked at her. Now I'm cursing myself for not going. I could have seen her, explained what happened.

"You didn't happen to get her number, did you?" I ask him hopefully.

"I thought you had her number."

"No. She changed it after I didn't call her. Worst mistake of my life not calling her back."

Riley shook his head sadly. "Damn. That sucks, man. I can see why you liked her, she's beautiful, down to earth and funny. I talked to her for a few moments before she was called away. Unfortunately, I didn't get her card but I might know someone who did. I'll ask around if you want.

"No. She's finally doing what she said she was going to do. I don't want to bring up her past. I'm happy for her."

"I still can't believe that she's the one who had you in your feelings like that. She was so nice."

I shrugged. "It's over now. I'm finally getting back in a good place and I'm ready to get back out there."

Riley nods towards the bar. "Maybe you should start over there. She's been checking you out for a while now."

I rolled my eyes and drank some of my beer. "Not that fast."

He laughed and we enjoyed the rest of our night laughing and drinking. We didn't bring Veronica back up, but she stayed on my mind the entire night.

"*I* got invited to go to Vegas!"

Chantel looked over her computer.

"What?"

"Remember the guy that I met at the showing?"

"You met a lot of people at the showing."

"The one that owns clubs in Vegas. He wants more paintings and wants to do a showing there."

"What! That's amazing, Ronnie! When?"

"Next week."

"For how long?"

"I'm not sure. He said possibly two months."

"Two months? Does he know you're pregnant?"

"I haven't told him but it's not like I'm going to be dancing in any of his clubs."

"Ronnie, you still haven't been to the doctor. I think you should postpone."

I rolled my eyes and groaned as I walked away from her.

"It's a chance to start over and who knows, I might just find a doctor down there."

"But we've never been apart. What am I supposed to do without you?"

"Come with me."

"I can't come with you, I have work."

"Chantel, you work from home, I'm pretty sure they have internet down there."

She looked like she was contemplating.

"Let me think about it because it's tempting."

"I already called my parents and they told me that if I don't go, I'll regret it forever."

"Damn, they're good. But they've always been supportive."

I wiggled my eyebrows at her and she laughed while giving me a dramatic eye roll.

"I'm not going to have you going somewhere where you don't know anyone and you're pregnant. I'll come."

I started dancing and that really made her laugh. *This was going to be great. I can always come back if I don't like it.*

CHAPTER 22

GREG

I walked into the office and sniffed the air. Deena was sitting at her desk and smiled at me as I walked in.

"What's that smell? It smells good." I asked looking around for candles.

"I bought some new wax melts. I thought we could use some good vibes in here."

"Yeah, smells good and it's relaxing."

"Good. Here you go." She handed me some papers.

"What are these?"

"Some of your clients want to come back. I guess the grass wasn't greener on the other side."

I could feel my face turning angry and my lip curl in disgust.

"I have half a mind to tell them to piss off. They left me when they didn't even have the full story and I'm just supposed to invite them back in?"

"You don't have to. You could always teach them a lesson."

"Yeah, but we don't have that type of luxury. I owe you a bonus, remember?"

"Oh, the bonus can wait. I'd rather see you smile again."

I put on a cheesy smile and she shakes her head.

"Riley called and said that he's going to be a little late. He's getting an oil change."

"Okay. I guess I'll go in here and make some calls. Wish me luck."

"You don't need it, you're amazing."

I winked at her and walked into my office. As soon as I plopped down in the chair, I looked at the messages. I closed my eyes and took a cleansing breath as I thought about making these phone calls.

I was on my third call when Riley walked in. I held up a finger as I finished the conversation.

"Yeah. No thank you for calling. No, no, there's no hard feelings. I look forward to seeing you next week."

After I hung up, I gave the phone two middle fingers and Riley laughed.

"Who was that?"

I handed him the papers and he looked through them.

"Are these your clients'?"

"Yep. They want to come crawling back. I told Deena that I should have said no."

"As your accountant, I'm glad that you didn't."

He sits down and gives me a look. Being friends with him for so long, I know that look.

"What did you do?" I interlocked my fingers and placed my hands on the desk so that I wouldn't wring his neck if it was something bad.

"I set you up on a date."

"Riley, no!" My hands now lay flat on my desk as I look at him exasperated.

"It's to late. Her name is Natalia and she's twenty-seven. I know how you don't like younger women, but she's almost thirty. She's beautiful and I'm going out with her friend Kita, so we can do this together."

"So, I'm a wingman now? God, she's probably the ugly friend."

"She's not, I promise. Kita showed me a picture of her and she's pretty."

"I hate you sometimes, Riley. When is this supposed date?"

"Friday."

I know better than to argue with him, so I just throw my hands up and nod.

"Whatever."

He smiles his successful smile and backs out of the office. I can only chuckle and shake my head.

CHAPTER 23

VERONICA- FOUR MONTHS LATER

"Ugh."

I stand up straight and stretch my back. I have been painting nonstop since I've been to Vegas. This three-week trip has turned into a full-time job. I glance over at Chantel in her office and she's hard at work on the computer. I don't know how I would have made it without her. She agreed to come here for a short time and we have been having a ball. I found us a cute four-bedroom house, right outside the city. The fresh mountain air was a great contrast to the lights and sounds of New York. I had a showing about a month ago and sold out within minutes. This promoter was good. Just by his words alone, he had people lined up for the showing. I could see why his fees were so high, he was worth it. Chantel was able to quit her job in billing and take over booking me for events and handling my finances. This baby has been growing rapidly and feeling her move was terrifying and exciting all at once. The doctor I found is a delight to work with and promised me that things were progressing normally. I was worried after I waited so long to go to the doctor but am excited that things were going as planned. I would love to have Greg here to share in this joyous moment but I feel it's too far gone now.

I hear footsteps behind me and I turn to look. Chantel walks in barefoot with a smile. She hands me a cup of tea and I take it eagerly.

"You look so cute today."

I look down at myself and frown. I have on a pair of large jean overalls with a sports bra. My belly is pushing the pockets of the overalls outwards.

"I don't have on anything special."

"Yeah, but pregnancy looks good on you."

I take a sip of the hot liquid and close my eyes with a moan.

"This is so good."

Chantel smiles and sits down on the couch. She looks at the painting that I'm working on and I see her eyes taking it in.

"That's darker than you usually paint. What's going on."

She knows me all too well. I always seem to paint my moods. A painting that starts out light and free will suddenly turn dark if I'm angry. I turn around and look at it while drinking my tea.

"I was thinking about Greg."

She was quiet and I turned back to her.

"You should call him."

I shake my head. "I can't. He would hate me if he found out this way."

"You never know."

"Yeah, no. Look where we are now. Life has been good to us and dealing with drama isn't good for me or the baby."

She shrugs and pulls her feet up on the couch. I can tell she doesn't like my answer but this isn't her decision. She quickly changes the subject.

"Well, don't forget that you have a meet and greet this weekend."

I roll my eyes. "How can I? You've reminded me every day."

"It's not my fault you forget everything."

I chuckle and place my cup on the side table. She knows that's her cue to leave as I begin letting the brush glide over the canvas. The tea will be long forgotten and cold by the time I finish painting for the night.

CHAPTER 24
GREG

"*V*egas! I am not going to Vegas. I have finally started getting showings again, I can't go to Vegas."

Deena clears her throat and I look over to her. She wags her finger at me and then looks to Riley then back at me.

"As someone who needs a vacation, I agree with Riley. Please go to Vegas and I'll go and see my grandkids. We all need a break and you've been working hard every day getting yourself back out of this rut, you deserve it. Hell, we all do."

I look over at Riley who has a shit-eating grin on his face and give him a dirty look.

"Fine."

"Yes!" He pumps his fist. "We are going to have so much fun, bro. Just let me handle everything."

"That's what I'm scared of."

Both Riley and Deena laugh and I can only whimper.

It's the weekend and I'm nervous and excited about going to Vegas. I look over at my girlfriend and smile. I cringe at the thought of saying that word. She was insistent that we label our relationship even though I told her that I wasn't ready to settle down. A couple of months ago, we went out on a double date with Riley and her friend. I could tell that she was clingy from the start and I should have put a stop to it then but seeing Riley happy and begging me to give it a try had me staying with her. She's nice and someone I could talk to, but she wanted me to fawn over her like Riley did with her friend and that's not me. I'm in my forties so our conversations weren't compatible sometimes. Where I wanted to talk about business, she wanted to talk about fashion. I'm not going to lie; she's tried to be very reassuring with all of the mess that I had going on in trying to get my business back on track, but I could tell that she was tired of hearing about it. I felt bad sometimes though because I find myself looking at her in dislike. It's nothing that she's done, it's who she is. Her voice is high, she wears a lot of makeup, she takes forever in the bathroom and she doesn't take much seriously. She hasn't spoken to me about her goals and has no idea about the significance of saving money. She lives her life in a freedom I've never had the privilege of living. She's been given everything in her life and is still supported by her parents. She's spoiled and everything is not funny. All of this comes down to, she is everything that Veronica was not. Yes, Veronica is younger than Natalia but our talks were different. We spoke of goals and where we saw ourselves in the future. We both started from a bottom and worked our way up. Our talks always meant something. I made love to Veronica one time and that one time has been seared into my brain. Making love to Natalia repeatedly is nothing comparable to that one time with Veronica. Ever since I felt Veronica's skin on mine, saw my hands on her hips, felt her lips on mine… I had been lost. I can close my eyes and picture the perfect dark skin under my hands. The thick curls running through my fingers and I'm on cloud nine. But, when I open my eyes, dark brown eyes aren't staring back at me. Don't get me wrong, Natalia is beautiful. She could be a model. Her eyes are blue, her hair is a chestnut brown, her features hold an exotic look to them and she turns heads wherever she goes. It's just not my head that's turning towards her. I've allowed myself to become comfortable with her and it's not fair to either of us. I want to say that she's growing on me but I'm not sure how far in the future I can see us going. I know that I'm holding on to her because I know the thought of being alone with my thoughts are worse. Sometimes, I grab my keys and go to the door and say, 'this is the day that I'm going to find her' but I have to remember, she's moved on and I'm trying to do the same.

Natalia looks over at me and catches me staring. She smiles and looks back at the road as she's driving.

"I think we are going to have a great time, don't you?"

I shrug and look out the window. "I hope so. The weather will be better for sure."

"Yes. I can't wait to feel some sun on my face."

I just smile at her excitement. Riley insisted on bringing Kita and Natalia was not to be left out. I thought this would be a trip for Riley and me, but he is in love and I certainly didn't want to be a third wheel. Hopefully, I can pull myself out of this funk before this trip is over.

The plane touches down and as soon as we step off the plane, the heat hits us square in the face. The girls take off squealing and holding on to each other while me and Riley grab the luggage. We catch a cab to the Luxor and take in the massive hotel. The women are still chatting excitedly as we walk in and get checked in. The rooms that Riley got us were exquisite and I was surprised. Sometimes he can be a clown and I find myself cleaning up his messes, but he did great this time. The view of the strip and the mountains were beautiful from our room and I couldn't wait to see it at night.

"Meet you downstairs at ten?" Riley calls over his shoulder as he walks to his door.

I nod and close the door to our room. It wasn't until I got into the room and actually looked out the window that I started to get excited about this trip. Natalia walks over and smiles before giving me a sultry look. She starts to unbutton her shirt and I raise a brow in approval. Her breasts sit high on her chest and rise and fall with each breath. I make my way closer to her and help to relieve her of the rest of her clothes. Although she's annoying, she still manages to get a rise out of me. As we lay in the bed, I make sure to take my time and kiss her all over, when I kiss in between the junction of her thighs, her legs clamp down on my ears. My ears ring as I slowly push them away until she explodes on my tongue. I grab a condom from my wallet and ready myself above her. Her body is moving in anticipation and I smirk. I position myself and slowly press in. As I seat myself all the way, she hisses. I pull back so that I won't hurt her and start a rhythm.

"Yes, just like that." She cries.

I close my eyes as her voice distracts me from my mission. I angle myself and she moves with me. I try to reposition her but she doesn't move and I start to get frustrated. I focus on the feel of her and her walls are pulsating and it doesn't feel good. She's trying to control our lovemaking and I'm getting more irritated. The more I try to position her body, she tries to arch or position her own way. It feels unnatural. I try to clear my mind and think of something that will bring me to the edge but I'm brought back to the present by nails digging into my back. I cry out and arch away from her and she takes that as a sign to continue. I quickly pull out and wiggle from her grasp as I turn her over. She rises up onto her knees and I hurry back inside of her before I lose my hardness. I grab her hips and pull her back to meet my thrusts. Her cries are getting louder and I shake my head to clear my thoughts. As I close my eyes, Veronica's face fills my thoughts. I see her smile, I hear her laugh, I feel her under me and I lose it. My thrusts become erratic and Natalia's moans are now a high-pitch shrill. Her body quakes and I seat myself as far as I can and my head falls backwards as I groan. I keep my eyes closed as she pulls away from me and I can feel her turn around. Her lips lightly kiss my chest. I don't want to open my eyes because when I do, I know that Veronica will disappear. As I feel Natalia start to fondle me, my eyes snap open and I pull away. She looks up at me with a hurt expression and I smile down at her.

"That was a long flight. How about we take a shower and I can wash you."

At the promise of my hands on her, she quickly smiles and scoots off the bed. *God, let this trip go by fast.*

CHAPTER 25

VERONICA

'm starting to loathe meet and greets. I'm cranky and I know it's the pregnancy. All I want is some avocado toast with a glass of apple juice. I have never eaten avocados so much in my life. At least my cravings are healthy. I chuckle at myself as I think about eating and Chantel gives me a look. I laugh at her facial expression and tell her that I'm okay. I look around at all of my paintings behind me and smile. The table is set up right in the middle of the room and I have prints of my paintings sitting in front of me. I start signing a couple to get ahead of the game while the promoters assistant puts up line placements up to keep the line under control. It's all about exposure and putting myself out there. I never realized how many art dealers there were in Nevada until I got here. I peek up to see a crowd growing outside the door and my stomach flutters. I'm still not used to be in front of crowds but I've sold so many paintings because of meet and greets. I'm currently working on special projects from my gallery in New York a couple of months ago as well as paintings to sell independently. Life has changed so much in just a short amount of time and I'm extremely grateful. I didn't even see Chantel walk out but she comes back with a bag of chips and a small container of

guacamole. My eyes light up and I forget the pen in my hand and trade it for the food. She sniggers and hands me an apple juice. My eyes water and I can feel my lip trembling.

"Oh god. Please don't start crying." She says as she rubs my back.

"I can't help it. I don't know where I'd be without you."

"Keep it together, Ronnie."

I nod my head not trusting my voice as I eat a chip. The promoter walks over and talks with Chantel as I down my juice. She smiles at whatever he says and the rope is moved for people to come in. I quickly wipe my mouth and smile as they approach the table.

It's like second nature. I answer questions and sign more prints. The line moves quickly and I even receive a couple of offers for more original paintings. As the line starts to dissipate, I start taking pictures with a couple of people with a backdrop of one of my more colorful pictures. I try to stand at an angle so that my stomach doesn't get in the way. I thought the promoter would be upset when he found out that I was pregnant but it's been wonderful. I've gotten more exposure since I've told him. I'm labeled as "limited" because of my current condition and people want access to me before I stop taking orders. *Tonight, wasn't as bad as I thought it would be. Me and Chantel will certainly celebrate afterwards.*

CHAPTER 26

GREG

*L*aughter could be heard as soon as the doors from the outside opened and the noise was comforting. My thoughts have been all over the place and the noise of the casino was a much-needed distraction. The ladies looked great and Riley and I were dressed casually in a pair of slacks and comfortable shirts. We walked around the strip and took in the sights as we gambled in multiple casinos. I had already spent over a hundred dollars on slot machines and have barely broken even. Natalia was doing great as she had already won over three hundred dollars. When we walked into one of the other hotels, we saw a line of people waiting for an event but didn't see what it was. I'm not one for lines so we hurried past and continued to gamble. My luck was changing because I just hit for a thousand dollars and told myself that I was done. I have made my money back and then some. I excused myself as they continued to play to go to the restroom. Natalia pouted like a child and I could only smile. It's not like she was using her own money. I walked back past the room that had a line and saw that the line was gone. I peeked in and saw some beautiful art pieces behind a table. There was no one seated at the table and I poked my head in further to see. My breath left me in an instant and I had to catch myself on the doorframe. Taking pictures in the corner was the face that haunted my dreams. *Veronica.* My heart hammered in my chest and I couldn't breathe. She looked so beautiful with her huge smile. She laughed at something someone said and I felt it in my bones. She gave the woman she took the picture with a hug and as they walked away, I saw something that I wasn't prepared for. Veronica was pregnant. My heart shattered into a million pieces. As her head swiveled towards me, I quickly backed out of the room and ran to the restroom. *Fuck, fuck, fuck.* I can't believe what I just saw. She has taken up so much space in my head that I never would have thought she would be pregnant. I had to close my eyes to contain the rage I felt as I pictured someone else's hands on her body. I didn't even want to go back out there but then again, I wanted to demand she tell me who the father was. This already aggravating trip just took a turn for the worse.

I knew that I couldn't hide in the bathroom forever. I fixed my face and went in search of Riley. They were all laughing and cheering as Natalia won another hundred dollars and I tried to put a smile on my face but Riley saw me before I could get myself together. He quickly walked to me and held me away from where the girls were playing.

"Hey, what's wrong?"

"Nothing."

"Greg. C'mon man."

I closed my eyes and sighed. "I just saw Veronica."

"Veronica? The painter? No fucking way. Here?"

"Yep, and she's pregnant."

"Greg, you're kidding." His eyes were large.

"I wish I was."

"Damn, bro. Did you talk to her?"

"Hell no." He looked at me in concern and I smiled. "I'm okay. It's a good thing really. It's closure."

"Damn, I'm sorry. You think this is why she disappeared? You should talk to her."

"Yeah. If that's the case, that means that baby could be mine."

"Damn, that would be messed up."

"I was with her months ago, there's no way. She's clearly moved on."

I saw Riley looking over my shoulder and turned to look. There were men carrying her art through the lobby and Veronica and another woman were all smiles as they followed in behind. The woman with her caught our eye and her eyes widened in recognition. I had never seen this woman before but she obviously knew me. I could feel my lip curl as Natalia came up behind me and draped herself over my shoulder and kissed my cheek. I pulled her close and never lost contact with the woman's eyes. Her face sneered and I could only cock my head in confusion. *Why would she be upset?* Veronica went to turn around and the woman put her arm through hers and hurried her out the door. Riley and I shared a look before we gathered the ladies and went to another casino. I had too much on my plate right now to deal with Veronica and why she left.

$\mathcal{M}$y heart hasn't stopped hammering in my chest and I'm starting to get worried. My head is pounding and I just want to make it through dinner. Riley keeps looking at me like I'm going to pass out any second. I wanted to walk up to her so bad and ask for an explanation but she looked so happy. *Who am I to mess that up for her? The more I think about her, the more I want to find her again. I'm miserable and she's happy, it doesn't seem fair.*

"Don't you think so?"

I look over at Riley and then at Natalia. Her face shows her uncertainty as she looks at me for an answer.

"I'm sorry, what?"

She looks annoyed. "The live show. Wasn't it nice?"

"Yes. I loved it."

Her smile looked forced as her and Kita shared a look between them. I had to get back in the moment. Veronica has already moved on and I need to do the same.

"Let's go dancing." I announce and the table looks at me with apprehension. I shrug. "What?"

Riley takes a drink of his wine and arches a brow. I look over at Natalia and she nods with a small smile. We finish eating and I'm actually looking forward to losing myself in some music. *How am I supposed to let her go?*

"*D*id you see how many pictures I signed! Tonight, was amazing."

I look over at Chantel who smiled even though it didn't reach her eyes.

"What is up with you? You haven't been right since we left the hotel."

Her eyes closed and when they opened, her face turned to the ceiling. I hurried next to her and sat down. I placed my hand on her knee concerned.

"What happened?"

When her eyes looked at me, they looked sad.

"I saw Greg." My hand moved from her leg and my head tilted in confusion as I waited for her to continue. "He was at the hotel and he was with another woman."

"What? Did he see you? Did he say anything? Why didn't you tell me?"

"He saw me but I don't think he knew who I was, but his eyes were on you. He looked hurt, confused and a little angry."

"Dammit. You think he's still there? You should have told me."

"I should have said something then but you were so happy

and I didn't want you to see him with that woman. I'm sorry, Ronnie. I was just trying to look out for you."

I pulled her into a hug. "Yeah, I know. I'm kind of glad that I didn't see him. See, this is another reason why I didn't tell him. He's with someone else. Could you imagine finding out your boyfriend had a baby on the way?"

"You're probably right but you can't keep this from him forever."

I let her go and took her hands. "I know but now isn't the time. Did he at least look happy?"

Her shrug told me everything I needed to know. I know I did the right thing… I hope.

CHAPTER 29
GREG

"Greg, please slow down."

My thrusts were coming faster and faster as I held Natalia's legs higher. I could only picture Veronica laughing and laying on someone else's chest. The anger I feel as the picture forms in my head has me blacking out.

"Please…"

I look down into the scared face of Natalia and I can feel my lip curl. This isn't her fault but she isn't who I want. I'm frustrated, hurt and angry. I climb up from her and storm to the bathroom and slam the door. I start the shower and ball my fists up in anger. *How dare she be happy. It was supposed to be with me. Is this all my fault because I left her alone and I didn't explain anything?* I scoff as I think about how she didn't waste any time in sleeping with someone else after me. I know we weren't together but I wanted her. My heart hurts and now I'm embarrassed because I just took my anger out on the woman, I'm supposed to be with. I step into the shower and let the hot water scorch my skin. I need to get it together. I need to use this as fuel. *She's moved on Greg, and it's time for you to accept that you will never be.*

We flew home the next day and Natalia barely spoke two words to me. I've apologized profusely and even though she accepted it, I feel that this relationship may be over. It was inevitable and I'm a little relieved. I explained what happed to Riley and he was sympathetic. I was ready to get home and lose myself in work. I knew that by the time I got back, I would have enough to keep me busy for a while. As great as it was to get away, this was not the vacation I had hoped for. I wish her well, but I have to let her go.

CHAPTER 30

"*W*hen are you going to stop? You're so close to giving birth and you haven't had time to enjoy it." Chantel asked.

I took a huge bite of my pizza and shrugged. "I have that show back in New York next month and I think I may take some time off after that."

"I hope so because I hate to tell you, but you look tired."

I absently rub my stomach. "I am tired. I'm ready to see my parents. They are ready to see their grand baby."

"I'm ready to see her too but I'm laughing inside at the thought of your parents. They weren't too excited a couple of months ago."

I groan and shake my head as I remembered how hard it was to tell them that I was pregnant. They didn't find out until I was four months along. My mother was surprised and my father was disappointed. They have always wanted the best for me and being a single mother was not in the plans. The fact that they were so happy that I was going to Nevada to live out my dreams and I knew that I was pregnant and didn't tell them, made it worse. Needless to say, they were worried on top of being disappointed. They had been married for so long and could see their only daughter being the same way. Then, the fact that I wouldn't tell them who the father was made things even more tense. It took months of apologizing and showing that I could make it on my own before they made peace with it. Now, the excitement of meeting their grand baby overshadows any scandal over how I got here in the first place.

I smile and look down at my protruding stomach. "I'm excited to see her face."

"Did you call Greg's office?"

"Yeah, but he wasn't there and his secretary said that she would give him the message. That was last month. I was hoping that I could talk to him before I got back to New York." *I didn't tell her that I left my name as Ronnie and not Veronica.*

"Well, at least you tried."

"Yep. Come on, help me up, I've got to pee."

Chantel laughed and stood up to pull my arms as I groaned. I could feel her eyes on me as I walked out of the room. She's been like a hawk lately. Ever since the day that she saw Greg, she's been checking in with me to make sure I'm okay. I still wish I could have seen him. I could have told him and tried to explain why I kept this baby a secret. I keep telling Chantel that I'm okay, but she never believes me. I even tried to show her I was okay by going out to dinner with a guy a couple weeks ago. It was a little awkward being pregnant and, on a date, but I still had fun. When I came back to the living room, she was standing in front of my latest painting. There was a lot of red on the canvas and I named it 'heartbreak'. The strokes were haphazardly splayed across and they looked angry and sad. Every time I looked at it, I felt the hurt that I allowed into my life and the joy of the life that that heartbreak gave to me.

"Do you like it?"

She looks over her shoulder. "I do but it looks... angry."

"It is but it's not finished yet. I'll try to bring some joy into it."

She still kept her back to me as she spoke. "I'm so proud of you. You're living your dream and I'm so glad that I get to be a part of it."

I walk up behind her and hug her as best I can without my stomach getting in the way.

"I'm glad you're here with me too."

CHAPTER 31

GREG

I slap the magazine down on Riley's desk and he picks it up. I'm on the cover and he smiles.

"Rising above it all. That's a nice headline."

"Right? I'm happy with how it turned out."

"I love it, man. We should go and celebrate your first comeback magazine cover."

"You're always looking for a reason to celebrate."

"Yep, so how about it?"

"Is Kita going to be there? I don't want to see her dirty looks. She is still pissed that I broke it off with her friend."

"She'll get over it. She's just looking after her friend."

"Yeah, by staring daggers at me."

"Let's not talk about them. Dinner?"

"Why not. I just signed another contract today and I couldn't be happier."

I look over at the many messages that I have yet to go through. Business has been good and there are more clients coming in every day.

"Good. Let's finish up here and I'll drive."

"Cool."

The restaurant was crowded. There was a bachelor party happening and I was annoyed already. The group was loud with laughter and yelling. I looked at Riley for help and he chuckled.

"Maybe we should go somewhere else." I offered.

"No. I love their gnocchi."

I groaned and followed him to the table. At least, we were on the other side of the room. I ordered a drink and listened to the yelling from across the room. The group finally left the restaurant after us being there for thirty minutes. I felt like I was finally able to breathe. Seeing happy relationships still made me jealous. That is until I looked up at the television screen and saw *her.* Looks like she was coming next month for another exhibit. I groaned and Riley turned to see what I was looking at. He closed his eyes and groaned with me.

"We should go." I tell him.

"No, we shouldn't."

"I think we should. I want to talk to her."

"And you think a working function is where that should happen?"

I shrugged and took a nice gulp of my drink. "I just want to speak to her and congratulate her on her success."

"It's not a good idea and I'm not going with you to watch you make an ass out of yourself."

"Whatever. I may not go either. It was just a thought."

"Well, put that thought out of your head. That woman does not want you."

I smiled slyly and rose my glass to him. *I'm going.*

CHAPTER 32

VERONICA

"Goddamn it's cold!"

We stepped off the plane and the jetway was freezing. I hurried my small jacket around me. The sun was shining when we had left Nevada and this was giving me the biggest reason, I was glad to be gone from New York. Chantel grabbed my carry-on and walked quickly into the terminal. At least the terminal had a little more heat.

"Come on, let's hurry up and get this rental." She exclaimed as she rushed me through the crowd of people.

I was breathing hard and the baby was lying on top of my bladder by the time we make it to where we were supposed to be. I let her pick up the rental while I found a bathroom. I made sure to call my parents to let them know that I was in town. I sent them tickets to the event and I couldn't wait to see them. When I went back to the rental place, Chantel was being handed a key and she smiled as we walked to find the car. They gave us a cute SUV and I let her drive. I yawned big and couldn't wait to get to the hotel to take a nap. The event wasn't until tomorrow and we had to make sure that the courier service had my paintings there. We shipped them off a couple of days before we left to come here to make sure they had enough time to make it. It felt good to be back in the city and you could definitely smell the difference in the air. Where New York air is heavy, the mountain air is crisp and light. I smiled as I heard the constant horns honking followed by the occasional person screaming, it was home. Chantel navigated the streets and made her way to the hotel that the event was taking place. I wanted to be as close as possible seeing as though I was so close to giving birth. I was so glad that I went to get my hair braided before we came. It was one less thing I had to worry about. With my natural hair always being out, I was surprised and excited to see that my hair has grown past my bra strap. I didn't want any kind of extra hair added because I was carrying around too much weight as it was. My simple straight back braids were cute and away from my face.

We get checked into our rooms and plan to get dinner downstairs at the restaurant after my nap. I was happy to be home but I will be glad when this is over. I promised Chantel and my parents that I would relax for these last couple of weeks and take it all in. I gave my best friend a hug and went into my room.

"*D*eena, were you able to get me tickets to that art event tomorrow?"

She opens her desk drawer and pulls out two tickets and hands them to me.

"Who are you taking?"

"My sister, Marissa. She loves art."

"Oh, that's nice. I hope you have fun."

I smile my thanks and walk into my office. I told Riley that I wasn't going but I needed to see her. Just one last time. I plop down into my chair and spin slowly. *I just hope that I don't screw this up. This could be my only chance.* I called my sister and offered to take her as a thank you gift for getting me out of that mess earlier this year. I'm finally starting to see a light at the end of the tunnel and I refuse to go back down that road again. I needed to let go of the past and move myself forward and with that, I've been thinking about selling my first building. It's just sitting there and now it holds memories that I'd soon rather forget. My phone rings to break me out of my thoughts and I thankfully answer.

~

The place was packed. There was camera's flashing every-where and private conversations being had all over. I guided my sister through the throngs of people and made it to a line of photographers.

"Mr. Devereux, over here! Mr. Devereux!"

I paused and took a couple of pictures while my sister watched from the side with a proud smile. I hurry past the rest as more people were coming behind me.

"Want something to drink?" I ask her.

"That would be great."

I nod and leave her for a second to go to the open bar. I waved to gather the bartender's attention and ordered two glasses of wine. With those in hand, I make my way back over to where I left her. It's a juggling act as I excuse myself in between people. I bump into someone and jump backwards as one of the drinks spill over.

"I'm sorry."

I turn to see who I bumped and the woman looks familiar. I can't place where I've seen her before but her face looks haunted. I smile and give a short nod at her before she takes off. I shake my head and finally make it back to where Marissa stood.

"This place is crazy packed."

"I know, I almost lost the drinks twice."

She smiled and sipped her wine while we watched people laughing and talking. A couple of people came and shook my hand but I'm glad that no one wanted to hold a conversation.

CHAPTER 34

VERONICA

"Ronnie, he's here." Chantel looked worriedly at me.

My stomach cramps and my eyes search the room but I don't see him. "Where?"

"He was over by the bar when I bumped into him."

"I can't let him get in my head right now. Maybe, I can avoid him and make it out of here unscathed."

"I hope so. There are way too many cameras here. We certainly don't want this to happen on camera."

I heard a squeal behind me and turned to see my mom walking over in a beautiful maroon dress. I had never seen my dad dressed up but he cleaned up very well. I hurry over and hug them both.

"I'm so glad you made it."

My mom held me close. "I wouldn't miss this for the world. I'm so proud of you, honey."

"Thanks mom."

I let her go and hug my dad.

"You look good baby girl."

"Thanks dad."

They both give Chantel a hug and she blows me a kiss as she takes them over to the table that I had reserved for them.

The lights start to dim and the main speaker walks up to the podium to gather everyone's attention. The crowd hushes and all eyes are on the raised stage. My art is featured behind him as he talks about me and how proud he is to have my art as a permanent fixture in the gallery. I could feel my eyes misting as I thought about how far I've come in just a short amount of time.

"You look beautiful."

I jumped at having a voice in my ear. Without turning around, I knew who was there.

"I can truly say that you followed your dream and I'm proud of you."

"Thank you." I whispered.

"I know your parents are proud too."

My eyes seek out my parents and Chantel but their focus is on the stage.

"They are."

"And the father?"

I turn around quickly while placing my hand on my stomach and look him in the eye.

"Yes. He said he's proud of me."

The smile on his face was fake and I could see hurt in his eyes.

"What about your girlfriend? How is she?"

"I don't have one."

My heart hammered in my chest at having him so close to me. My body knew his even if it was just once.

"The one that you were with after you left me without a word. The one that you were with at the fire."

I could see his brain trying to work back to those moments and as he was about to speak, I interrupted.

"Greg, there's something I need to tell you…"

A light tap on my elbow made me turn around and a little

lady was pointing to the stage. The speaker was staring at me and my eyes rounded and I turned back to Greg.

"I'm sorry, I have to go. I do have to talk to you. Wait for me?"

He nodded and I quickly walked up the two stairs and to the podium. The applause was loud and I made the speech prepared for me. When I was through, the room stood and clapped and I was helped down from the stage. My parents were there with tears in their eyes and hugged me. I looked around for Greg but I didn't see him. I was whisked away to take questions and the night proceeded without me getting to speak with him. I could still smell his cologne if I closed my eyes. My time in New York was short so I hoped I could see him again before I left.

CHAPTER 35
GREG

I thought that I could do it. That I could casually speak to her without wanted to grab her and take her with me. The confirmation that she was still talking to the baby's father cut me deep. She told me to wait but when the speeches were over, I took my sister and left. I could only kick myself as I thought back to the fire and what she must have seen. I was with my sister all day and I know that's who she saw with me. This whole time I could have explained this to her but I had let too much time pass by. She smelled so good and she looked beautiful. Whatever healing I had done to my heart was ripped open at seeing her. She was right in front of me and I wanted to kiss her. The way her eyes went to my lips as I spoke. When I dropped my sister off, I went home and poured me the biggest glass. I plopped down on the couch, still in my suit. I shouldn't have gone. Riley was right, and I'll never tell him that to his face. I wasn't ready to see her. Now that I have a fresh picture in my head of her, it's all I see when I close my eyes. My phone rings on the counter but I don't want to talk to anyone.

∽

Deena

I got a call on the emergency line that there was someone in the building downtown. I have been trying to call Greg but he isn't answering. I would call the police but the last time someone went in there, they didn't even care. The building has been vacant for years and they run people away from over there all the time. I'll leave him a message and hopefully he listens.

CHAPTER 36
VERONICA

After the night was finished and everyone left, I told Chantel that I was going to bed but I snuck away and caught a cab a couple of blocks away. The building that we had our rendezvous at was just around the corner. I thought how amazing it would be if I went there and he just happened to show up. Surprisingly the door was open and I peeked in. There were no lights this time and it looked scary. Creaks and groans sounded as I poked my head in and contemplated if I should just leave. If I got killed, no one would even know that I was there. I had on my sneakers and I went against my better judgement and hurried to the elevator. The doors opened right away and I pressed the button for the top floor. As soon as I walked out onto that rooftop, it was all worth it. The stars were bright and there were no clouds in the sky. The air was cold and I pulled my scarf and coat around me. I closed my eyes and sent out a silent prayer hoping that he would show up. I needed him to know the truth, not just for me, but for the baby also. I didn't want to have this baby without him knowing. Thinking about the smell of his cologne and the huskiness of his voice sent shockwaves to parts of my body that had lay dormant. The night air was cold and I didn't want to get sick so I stayed for a while longer before I hurried back inside to leave. I was sad and lonely and knew of only one person to help me alleviate that. Chantel has been great but I miss being held. The way his hands landed on my hips at the event had my heart racing. I wanted so badly to lay my head back on his shoulder and let him hold me. I didn't feel right dating or let alone, sleeping with someone while I was pregnant, so thoughts of Greg were all that I had to keep me going. As I stepped off the elevator, I heard a noise inside the darkness. Not wasting any time, I hurried as fast as I could with my swollen feet, back out into the cold. The cab was still sitting there and assured me that no one had come in through the door. He took me back to the hotel and I went to bed. I left a note on the table on the rooftop just in case he showed.

I miss our meetings at midnight.
Love V

CHAPTER 37
GREG

My head was pounding and as I looked on the table, the bottle was half gone. I was still in my suit and had fallen asleep on the couch. I scrubbed a hand down my face and stretched. I retrieved my phone and saw the missed call from last night. I listened to the message from Deena and rolled my eyes. *That building is becoming a nuisance and I need to sell it.* I took a shower and shaved my face before getting dressed. *I'll go and check on the building and then go to work.*

When I pulled up in front, the door was cracked open. I shook my head and grabbed my flashlight. As I walked in, there didn't seem to be anyone in there. I rode the elevator to various floors and there was no one around. When I got to the roof, I could feel my lip curl in aggravation. I hated coming here now because the memories of laughter and conversation assaulted me each time. The table still sat in the same spot and there were two glasses that sat there also. I walked over and my brow furrowed. I stopped dead in my tracks when I saw the piece of paper laying on the table. I was scared to move it or read it. My steps were heavy as I approached the table and willed my eyes to look down. When I did, my heart sank. *She was here.*

I miss our meetings at midnight.
Love V

She came for me and I was drunk. I tried to think of where she could be. *Did she leave town yet?* I took the piece of paper and placed it in my pocket and ran down the hallway to the elevator. I drove as fast as I could back to the hotel where the event happened the night before. Maybe they knew where she might be. When I arrived at the front desk, the woman behind the counter was all smiles.

"Hi, how can I help you?"

"Um, I'm looking for someone."

"Okay, maybe I can help. Do you have a meeting in the conference room?"

"No. I'm looking for someone who was here last night. The artist, Veronica Mason."

"Oh, I'm sorry. I can't give you any information about any guests."

"Can you at least tell me if she is still here?"

"I'm sorry, I can't."

"Dammit. Okay, thank you."

She smiled nervously as I walked away. I had no idea in what to do.

CHAPTER 38

CHANTEL

I couldn't take it anymore. Ever since we came back from New York, things have been going downhill. Veronica woke up this morning and I could tell she had been crying. Every time I ask her what was wrong, she keeps saying nothing. I saw when Greg walked up to her at the event last week and I was hopeful that she would finally tell him. When I saw him stride off with a hurt expression, I knew that she hadn't. She's been moping around and her paintings have become darker. The rest that she said she was going to have, is nonexistent. I'm at a loss and it looks like I need to take matters into my own hands. I go to my office and begin to type.

Mr. Devereux,

You don't know me but I've seen you before, I'm Veronica's best friend, Chantel. I know this letter is coming from left field but I feel that you may be the only person to help me with a situation. Veronica is going through something major at the moment and she needs to speak to you. I'm placing our address at the bottom of this letter and maybe if you have the time, you could fly here and speak with her. I would tell you to call her on the phone but I think an in-person visit would be best. I'm sorry if this letter is confusing and not in full detail but I wouldn't be a great friend if I didn't try to help her.

Thank you for your time,
Chantel

I find his business email address and hit send. There's no turning back now and the ball is in his court. Hopefully, she doesn't kill me when she finds out what I did. I peek back out and I can see her staring out of the front window. It's getting harder and harder to watch someone who was just full of life a week ago, withdraw into themselves. Hopefully he reaches back out.

I searched high and low for any sign of Veronica after her showing. I asked the event planner if he had any information on her and I guess with the aggressiveness in which I was asking, no one would give me any info on her. I have thrown myself into work and if I stay busy, I have no time to think about those beautiful brown eyes, the way her breath hitched when I placed my hands on her hips, the smell of her perfume, or the way she stared at my lips as I spoke. I'm sitting at dinner with some of my clients and Riley and it's so hard to concentrate. It's been weeks since I've seen her and the most that I've found out is she's still in Vegas somewhere. That place is way too busy to be looking for a person in. Plus, she's probably about to or already had her baby. I check my phone and scroll through my emails. There's nothing new and I was about to put my phone away when I saw the spam folder. I usually just empty it because it's nothing but ads but something told me to open it. As I'm scrolling, I shake my head and question why I even opened it, then I see something. It's an email from someone named Chantel and it looked personal. It could be a potential client so I open it up. My heart sinks and I stand up unexpectedly. The people at the table look at me in shock and Riley stands with me looking concerned.

"Um, I'm sorry. I have to go."

Riley grabs my arm and looks at me like I've grown two heads.

"Greg, what is your problem?" He hissed.

I show him my phone and understanding dawns on his face.

"Go. I've got this."

I give him a grateful look and apologize as I hurry out of the restaurant. I can hear Riley in the background making excuses for me.

"You know how busy he is. Let's finish dinner and I'll gladly take the contracts back to the office."

I didn't stay around to see what their answers were. I got in my car and hightailed it home to get on the computer. I pulled up the airlines to see what was available and there was nothing until the morning. I hurried a bag together and booked the first flight out. This could either make me the happiest man ever or the dumbest.

I have never willed a plane to fly faster in my whole life. When we landed, I pushed past the people walking slowly and hurried to find a rental. Luckily with this being Vegas, there were plenty of cars available since people usually took the hotel shuttles. I put the address shown in the GPS and set off. The drive took me a little over a half hour and I was glad to see that the house wasn't near all of the hype of Vegas. The community was small and the mountains behind the houses were massive. There was a haze in the air that made the houses look like water in the distance. I pulled up to the house and my stomach was in knots. *What if she didn't want to see me? That email*

was weeks ago. I didn't care. I got out the car and hoped for the best.

CHAPTER 40

VERONICA

I got out of the shower and put on my stretch pants and my large shirt. I had been having small contractions and I was nervous. I had just two weeks until my actual due date and I was ready to meet her. There was a knock at the door and I groaned. Chantel was at the store picking up some food and I had just sat down. I pushed myself to stand and waddled to the door. When I opened it, I almost fainted. He caught my arm as my body stumbled backwards.

"Greg." His face was full of concern. "What are you doing here?"

He shook his head. "I have no idea. I just know that I needed to see you and if you tell me to go, I will."

I was in disbelief. How did he know where I was?

"Come in."

I backed up and he walked in slowly. I invited him to sit down on the couch and I stood. I didn't want to be trapped on the couch and struggle to get up if I needed to walk away.

"I'm so confused, how did you find me?"

"I got an email with the address."

"Who would do that?"

"It was signed, Chantel."

I was going to kill her. She could have at least warned me that this was a possibility.

"Oh my god, and you just hopped on a plane and came here?"

"Yeah."

"Why?"

"I wanted… no, needed to see you. You have no idea how hard it was seeing you. I thought we had something good going and then…"

"Then you left me. No explanation or anything."

"I know and that will haunt me for the rest of my life. Everything went to shit and I didn't know where to start. By the time I came looking for you, you were gone."

"I thought we had something too and then you didn't call, I was angry. I saw you on television afterward at that building with that woman and I freaked out. The way you were with her looked too familiar and I refused to be the other woman in any situation. Then I found out that I was pregnant and I didn't know what to do or how to tell you."

"Woman? That woman was my sister. She's also my lawyer." He paused and his head cocked to the side. "Wait… Are you telling me that this baby is mine?"

I looked away and he stood up suddenly. He took my arms and placed his face in my sight.

"Please tell me... Is this baby mine?"

I could only nod. He let me go and I felt the absence of his hands immediately. I looked over and he had his back to me.

"I'm sorry. I wanted to tell you but there wasn't a chance too."

When he turned around his face was hard.

"Wasn't a chance! You had ample time to tell me. Nine months to be exact. I've seen you multiple times and you chose not to tell me."

"I know. You were with someone and I didn't want to intrude…"

"Intrude! Veronica, it's a baby! That's not intruding. I had a right to know."

"I know, I'm sorry-I"

The contraction hit out of nowhere and I doubled over in pain.

"Ow."

His hand was back on my arm gently.

"What's happening? Are you okay?"

I nod my head and point to the couch. He helps me to sit down and I rub my stomach.

"Contraction."

The garage door opens and Chantel walks through the door.

"Hey, there's someone's car parked out front."

Her eyes meet Greg's and she fumbles the bags she's holding.

"He got our address from an email." I spat out.

She had the nerve to look guilty. Her face quickly changed as she took in my face.

"What happened? What's wrong? What did you do to her?"

He began to fumble over his words and I saved him the trouble.

"I had a contraction. Just one big one though."

She gave Greg a chiding look and he looked back at me.

"He knows. I told him."

Chantel sucked in a breath and tried to gauge his mood.

"Are you okay?" She asked me.

"Yeah. I think I need to lay down though."

She placed the bags in the kitchen and never took her eyes from Greg as she approached. She helped me to stand and I had to stand still for a minute to get my bearings.

"Walk me to my room."

Chantel started to come but I shook my head and pointed at Greg. She put her hands up and backed away.

"You'd better call for me if you need me."

I smiled over my shoulder and nodded.

CHAPTER 41

GREG

I'm going to be a father. I'm on autopilot as I walked slowly behind Veronica as she went into a large bedroom. My brain still hasn't processed what she just told me. I look at her as if I'm seeing her for the first time as I helped her to sit on the bed and push herself back onto the mounds of pillows. She pats the bed beside her and I sat down apprehensively. I don't know what to do with my hands and I clasp them in my lap.

"I wish I would have known. I would have been there for you."

Her eyes closed and when they opened, there were tears. Wanting so badly to wipe them away, I choose to sit and wait for what she has to say. The room was silent but I swore I heard my heart beating.

"I wanted to tell you so many times and each time I thought about it, something happened. It just never felt right."

I could be angry, in fact, I was a little but she didn't need that. I sat back with her and placed my arm around her and she placed her head down on my shoulder. She turned her body and placed an arm around my stomach and I closed my eyes. I held her in silence as I tried to comprehend what was happening. She's been doing this all alone and as angry as I was, I had to see how strong she was for doing that. If I really process what was going on, I could tell her that she did the right thing by not telling me. It's hard for me to accept that but when I was going through my financial crisis and I had known I was going to be a father, I know that I probably would have pushed her away. I couldn't even think for myself, let alone a woman with a child. As much as I am angry about not knowing, I'm grateful to know now. I'm able to take care of her and the baby now that my client list is bigger than ever. I smile as I hold her close to me.

"So, now that I know, when are you coming back to New York."

Her body stiffened and she sat up with a perplexed look on her face.

"I'm not coming back to New York. I have work here."

I sat up and looked at her.

"But Veronica, you're having my kid."

"Yes, and I'm staying here."

"Are you serious? That's not fair."

"What's not fair? Me staying and doing the job that I love? You think that just because you know now that I'll throw myself at you and let you whisk me away back to the city? No."

"How am I supposed to go home knowing you're here with my child? Speaking of, is the baby a boy or a girl."

"A girl."

"Does she have a name or am I too late for that as well."

Her chin wobbled and she closed her eyes.

"I never asked you to come here."

"No, you didn't. You were going to allow me to go on with my life without knowing that I had a kid. Now, that's not fair."

"I think you should go."

"I don't think I should. We need to talk."

"This talking is draining and it's only leading to shouting."

"Whose fault is that."

She sucked in a breath and I regretted it instantly.

"Please leave."

"Veronica…"

"Now." She growled.

I closed my eyes and sighed. This was not how I envisioned this going. I nodded once and quickly got up from the bed and walked out of the room. I passed her friend in the kitchen and she gave me a look as I hastily made my way to the door.

"Is she okay?"

I shrugged and shook my head as I walked out.

CHAPTER 42
VERONICA

I wanted to call him back into the room so badly but my pride wouldn't let me. None of this was his fault and I knew my words hurt him. I watched the defeat in his stance as he waited for me to change my mind. I knew that I should have told him months ago but I wasn't prepared for this. The condemnation in his face as he spoke to me. I wanted him to be excited and fall into my arms with awe and gratitude that he finally knew. This isn't a movie though and things like that don't happen. When Chantel peeked into my room, I let the tears flow. She climbed onto the bed and hugged me.

"He was so angry, Chantel, and it's all my fault."

"It's okay. He knows now and it's up to him to come to terms with it. He needed to know and what's done is done."

"You think he'll come back? I said some ugly things to him."

"He hasn't left. He's still sitting out front."

My heart skipped and I looked at her.

"Go." She smiled "Talk to him."

I managed to climb out the bed and put on my slippers. I hurry to the door and when I open it, he's sitting in his car and turns towards me. His car door opens and he steps out with a troubled look on his face.

"Are you okay." He asks nervously.

I don't say anything, just keep walking towards him. He skips around the car and stands on the sidewalk. When I'm standing in front of him, I look up into his face.

"I'm so sorry, Greg."

His hands come to my face and hold my cheeks. He bends down and his forehead touches mine and we just stand there.

"I want to scream and curse but I also don't want to lose you again." He whispers.

"I know. You have every right to be upset with me."

"No. I'm hurt for sure but I'm glad that you didn't tell me."

I pulled away and looked at him.

"I wasn't in the right headspace to handle this news and you knew it. You kept it from me and if I had known, I'm not sure how I would have reacted. I'm glad that I know and I know that it's going to suck having you away from me, but we will work it out."

When he put his arms around me, I melted against him. He leaned back and bent down to kiss me. When our lips met, I was instantly back on that rooftop. He held me close as he worshipped my mouth. I sighed as we disengaged and then my water broke.

CHAPTER 43

GREG

*E*verything happened all at once. One minute we were standing in front of her house and now, she's being rushed to the hospital. I drove my rental and I am so glad to have gotten the extra insurance because they would have sent me a hell of a clean up bill. When we arrive at the hospital, they were only going to allow one of us to be with her and she started to cry. I wasn't going to stand in the way of the one person that she's had by her side but she was insistent.

"No! I need Chantel but he's missed so much already. I can't do this without them both."

The doctors didn't want to argue because the baby was ready and they didn't have time. They conceded and we were rushed to the back with her. In the middle of this chaos, I saw my life flash before me. I have been at the top, at the bottom, sad, lonely, but nothing could prepare me for seeing something that I helped to create take it's first breath. I watched in awe as doctors and nurses came in and out of the room and then when it was time, they told her to push. I was frozen in my spot beside her bed and my eyes could not believe what they were seeing. Her stomach was large as she lay with her feet splayed and then a tiny human was presented. I kissed her forehead and watched in amazement as they lay my daughter onto her chest. Veronica's hand held onto mine until she placed both of her hands on the baby's back. The baby's tiny cries that led to a wail warmed my heart. She had a full head of hair and her pale skin looked pink as they wiped her down. I was speechless. It was like the world moved while I stood still as I distantly heard voices around me as I watched the constant movement of the room. *How could I leave her? How could I leave this beautiful baby?* I was beginning to get lightheaded.

"Sir, are you okay?"

I looked into the eyes of a concerned nurse and I could only nod my head. She smiled and pointed to a chair next to the bed.

"Why don't you have a seat, I know this can be overwhelming."

I still didn't speak as I slowly sat down in the seat. I glanced up at Veronica and her friend and looked at the way they both laughed and cried tears of joy. I felt like an interloper. This woman that has been my every thought has just changed my life forever. My ears were ringing with all of the excitement that had just transpired. I sat with my head in my hands as I tried to process what just happened. My brain was moving so fast and it came to a complete halt as I saw a pair of shoes in front of me. I looked up and a nurse stood before me with a tiny bundle in her hands. I looked over at Veronica and she had tears streaming down her face. She nodded softly and I sat straight up and had little time to prepare as the nurse lay her in my arms. It was awkward at first and then as I looked down into her perfect face, it was like she had been there all along. She was so fragile and she belonged to me. Her face started to blur as I felt my tears pooling.

"She's absolutely perfect." I say to no one in particular.

My arms didn't know what to do as the nurse came and removed the baby from my arms so they could check her out and I stood up and cleared my throat. I straightened my shirt and shuffled my feet as Veronica and her friend looked over. I slowly approached her bedside.

"Veronica… I truly appreciate you allowing me to be a part of this beautiful moment. I only came down here to speak to you about what happened and I received so much more. I don't know if anything in my life could ever top this."

Her smile was sincere as she took my hand and squeezed.

I called Deena and told her what was happening and she cleared my schedule for the week. I stayed in Nevada until Veronica was sent home. I helped her to get settled and knew that my time with them was coming to an end. As she began getting into a rhythm, I watched as the two best friends worked as one. As bad as my heart hurt to leave, I put a smile on my face and kissed her gently before bidding my goodbye's. I held my daughter, whom we named Lyana, which means sun in Greek. I kissed her little cheek and promised her that I would be back. As I passed her to her mother, my heartstrings pulled a little more. *This child will never want for anything in her life if I could help it.*

The flight home was long and I let the tears fall without a care of who could see. Riley met me at the airport and one look at my face had him pulling me into a hug. I had my car there but he knew that I wouldn't be good to drive. I left New York a lonely man and came back a father. I showed him pictures and like a true best friend, told me how beautiful she was. This was by far the hardest thing I've had to do, leaving both of them behind.

CHAPTER 44

VERONICA- THREE MONTHS LATER

I've spoken with Greg over FaceTime just about every day. The way he speaks to Lyana as if she could hold a conversation back was adorable. I promised that I would bring her up soon. He was super busy with work and even mentioned that he was going to sell his building. He wanted to make sure that his daughter had everything she would need for college and more. I had sold more paintings and if I didn't want to work, I didn't have to. I'm getting paid to have my work placed in galleries all over and the money has been constant. Chantel could see how badly I wanted Greg to be around and pushed me to go and see him. She wanted to see her parents and I knew that mine wanted to see their grand-daughter. I didn't tell her or anyone about what I had been doing behind the scenes though. I had been in contact with Greg's secretary about his building that he was selling and I was going to buy it. I know how much that building meant to him and I wouldn't let him give that up. So, as soon as it was put on the market, I bought it. She was the only person that knew. I couldn't wait to get to New York. Of course, I wanted to see my parents but I had an idea that I needed to see through.

Lyana did amazing for her first flight. She was almost four months and slept the whole way. Greg picked us up from the airport and Chantel kissed me and the baby on our cheeks before she retrieved her rental to go and see her parents. Greg insisted that we stay with him and I was a little nervous. This was the first time that I was seeing his place. It's so crazy to think that we only slept together once and have now become a family. We talked like we've known each other for a long time while we were on the phone but the truth is, we have only spent a handful of wonderful days together before this whole baby episode.

His apartment was beautiful. Just outside Central Park and his view was one to be rivaled with. The streets were filled with people walking or jogging. As we walked up the stairs, he smiled at me and it was the smile that I have grown to love. The space was open and clean. The curtains were pulled back from the huge window in the living room to let in all of the natural light. It certainly didn't look like anyone lived there.

"Make yourself at home."

I looked around at the crisp apartment and wondered how he was going to keep a baby here. I followed him as he took our bags to a room down the hall. When he opened the door, I took in a breath. There was a beautiful nursery with a crib and a twin bed. There was a rocking chair in the corner and balloons painted on the wall. What really caught my attention was the large sun above Lyana's crib. Her name was in wooden blocks through the sun. I looked over at him in wonder and he had an embarrassed look on his face.

"Deena may have helped me a little." He looked around. Okay, a lot."

I chuckled. "It's beautiful."

"May I?"

He held his hands out and I placed the baby in his arms. She chose that moment to open her eyes and it was then I noticed that they shared the same eyes. Her dark curls were full all over her head and he rubbed his cheek across them. The smile she gave made my heart melt.

The first night, I slept in the room with the baby but the second night, I had to see him. I tiptoed out of the room so that I wouldn't wake her and crept to his room. The door creaked as I opened it and he sat up.

"Are you okay?" He asked. "Is the baby, okay?"

"We are fine."

I could feel his nervousness in the dark. The moonlight shone on the bottom of the bed and made it easier to find him in the dark. I sat down next to him and let out a breath.

"I'm sorry to wake you, I had to see you."

"I wasn't asleep."

I closed my eyes and let out a breath. "You can tell me to leave if you want to." I whispered.

He was quiet and when I looked up, there was a small smile on his face.

"I didn't know what or how to approach you so, I'm glad that you're here. I've been going crazy."

"I've missed you."

The corners of his mouth turned up as he leaned over and kissed me.

"It's been so long and I have thought about you so many times."

"I know, I've missed you to. I want to see you." He says as he looks down at my clothes.

I slowly stood up and lifted the shirt from my head. He swung his legs over the side of the bed and placed his hands on my hips. He pulled me forward and kissed my stomach. I still had not lost a lot of my baby weight and was still self-conscious. He didn't mind it at all as his tongue snuck out and tasted my skin. I ran my hands through his hair as he pushed my pants and panties down in one swoop. I closed my eyes and let myself live in the moment. His fingers expertly glided across my skin and I closed my eyes to feel each movement.

"We need protection. As much as I love our daughter, I'm not ready for another one."

He reached into the drawer beside the bed and placed a condom on. When he entered me, we both let out a groan. It turned me on even more to see him watch himself going in and out of me. His rhythm was steady and it all felt amazing. As he placed his body down on top of mine, our lips met as he sped up his pace.

"I'm never letting you go; I hope you know that."

I cried out into his mouth as his hips stilled and we lay panting.

"I wish you could stay." He whispered into my ear.

I felt a lone tear fall from my cheek as I closed my eyes. I couldn't answer him because I wanted to stay.

CHAPTER 45
GREG

*H*er skin was so soft. As I kissed her and heard her breathing increase, I knew I would not make it if I wasn't inside her soon. I stood and spun her around as I took my pants off and followed her into the bed. Her hands went under my arms and pulled me towards her and she kissed me. Her legs spread to give me room and lay as close as possible to her.

"We need protection. As much as I love our daughter, I'm not ready for another one."

I smiled down at her and opened the drawer beside my bed. I placed the condom on and took my place back between her legs. Her fingernails lightly moved up my sides and I shivered. I lined myself up with her and looked into her eyes as I pressed forward. Watching her hooded eyes close as I pressed forward was a beautiful thing to watch. I held my place until her eyes opened back up. As she looked at me, I began to move slowly.

"I'm never letting you go; I hope you know that."

The smile that creased the corner of her mouth told me that she knew that I wasn't playing. This is what I've been missing. The more that we've talked, the more I found myself wanting to be closer to her. It's always been her since the day that I saw her at the bank, it was her. I knew it as I looked into her eyes. Our love making wasn't hurried, we just took our time and enjoyed each other. When I felt that she needed relief, I took her leg and moved it to my opposite forearm. Her voice cracked as my skin met hers. I fastened my pace and brought us both over the edge. I let gravity remove me from her as I tried to hold on as long as I could. I got rid of the condom and pulled her back to my front. I glanced at the baby monitor that I turned on and saw our child sleeping soundly before I closed my eyes. *I'm never letting her go.*

I went to work missing her already. She took the baby to visit her parents and wasn't coming back for a couple of days. When I walked into the office, Riley and Deena stood with wide smiles.

"So? How'd it go?" Deena asked excitedly.

"Everything was perfect. She was perfect, the baby is perfect and I'm going to miss them both when they leave."

"Couldn't convince her to stay, huh?" Riley asked.

"I wish but no."

"Well, I for one, can't wait to hold that baby." Deena crossed her arms across her chest in a self-hug.

"Soon. Maybe, when she comes back from her parents."

They both smiled as I made my way to my office. Riley followed me in and leaned against the doorjamb.

"So, what really happened?"

My brow furrowed. "Nothing. We just talked and I've been enjoying my daughter."

"It's so weird to hear you say, daughter."

I chuckle. "I know. I'm still getting used to it."

A paper caught my eye and I picked it up.

"What's this?"

Riley shrugged. "Deena told me to put it there. Someone bought your building."

I closed my eyes and sighed. I was hoping no one would buy it and I would change my mind and keep it. Since I've been talking to Veronica, I couldn't help but think about our time on the rooftop.

"Shit."

"What? Having second thoughts"

I shake my head. "No. It's too late now. Plus, it's time to let it go."

CHAPTER 46

VERONICA

My parents shooed me out of the house quickly. I didn't tell them about Greg until after the baby was born. They were both shocked. Gregory Devereux is a name that all of the tri-state area knew and to know that he was their granddaughters father took them off guard. My dad actually drove to the city to meet Greg in person and talk with him. They hit it off well and after sitting down with him, Greg got his full blessing. My parents have always been old fashioned and me having a baby like this was not in the cards. Now that they have met him and heard the way I had been falling for him, they were all a go for us. After I told them of my plan about the building, they of course, wanted to watch the baby. I quickly caught the first Amtrack back to New York. I still hadn't told Greg that I bought his building and my stomach was in knots with anticipation. Deena had been a godsend in helping me through purchasing and finalizing everything. As soon as she brought Greg's attorney sister on board, it really worked out. We were able to purchase the building under my business name and he would never know who the owner truly was. As the train wound its way up the tracks, I thought about what I had planned. I had Deena buy some wine and a light spread of some kind and have it taken to the rooftop of the building. My plan was to sneak into town and surprise Greg. I smiled as I pictured the look on his face. I had less than an hour left on this train and I could put my plans in motion.

CHAPTER 47

GREG

I got off from work and wasn't looking forward to going home alone. She's only been in town for a couple of days and gone for one, but I missed her. When I opened the door, the silence hit me hard. I had grabbed me some take-out on the way home and sat it on the counter as I went to get in the shower. I dressed in a pair of sweats and a tank top. The night was wearing on and I wanted to call her but didn't want to seem pushy. We literally talk every night now. There was nothing on television and when I called Riley, he didn't answer the phone. It was going on ten o'clock when I cleaned the kitchen and grabbed me a bottle of water before heading to my room. My phone chimed and I took it from my pocket to look at the screen. My cheeks hurt from the smile that was on my face. There was a text on the screen from Veronica.

Meet me at this address at midnight

CHAPTER 48
GREG

That address was one that I know all too well and I have never dressed so fast in my life. *She was back in New York and didn't say anything? How in the hell did she get into the building?* I grabbed my keys and ran out the door. My worry level was high because I knew that the building just sold and she shouldn't be there if there were new owners. The place should have been sealed tight with new locks. That's all I needed was for her to go to jail for trespassing. I was going to get there before midnight, but I didn't care. My smile never left my face as I pulled up to the parking behind the building. I was angry and scared that she was here alone at night. When I walked in, there were lights on the floor that led to the elevator and I barked out a laugh. *She really recreated our first night.* I tightly griped my keys in my pocket as I rode the elevator up to the top level. My steps were brisk as I walked down the hallway. When I opened the door, she stood there looking over the edge. She wore a long sundress that blew in the breeze of the night. She turned at the sound of my footsteps and looked at her watch.

"You're early."

I shook my head at her and took her in my arms.

"What am I going to do with you? What are you doing here?"

"Do you like it?"

I was confused. "Like what?"

She smirked. "My building."

I let her go and looked at her shocked.

"It was you? You bought this place? How?"

"I had a little help."

I couldn't believe it. I hugged her tight and whispered in her ear.

"Thank you."

I kissed her and she pulled away and put a handout towards the table. I laughed and nodded as I took the seat she offered. As I sat down, she walked to the other side.

"Wine?"

I shrugged. "Why not?"

I watched her and bit my bottom lip as she poured us both a glass. I held my glass up to hers and they clinked together.

"You're so goddamned beautiful."

Her smile was radiant as she took the seat across from me.

*S*uccess. His face was everything that I imagined it would be. The look of surprise and gratitude looked good on him. I needed him to feel how that first night felt to me.

"Where is the baby?"

"With my parents. They all but kicked me out the house when I asked them to watch her."

He barked a laugh. "I missed this."

"I did too."

I turned on some music and I stood up and placed my hand out for him. He smiled his beautiful smile and took my hand and stood. We danced and I lay my head on his chest. The more I'm with him, the more I want to stay. We stayed there for about two hours before he drove us to his place. Without the baby there, we made up for lost time. We made love like we would never see each other again and my body was tired by the time we finished. We took a shower together and made love once again. His kisses were like magic and when we stepped out from the shower, he rubbed my back until I drifted off to sleep. I woke up to light kisses down my back as he entered me from the back. At this point, if another baby came from this, I wouldn't even care. We went to breakfast and he drove me to Philly to pick up the baby. Driving was much longer and the tolls were horrible getting through but being with him was worth it. My parents loved him and was glad to see us together. We ate dinner with them and made the drive back to New York and it felt like we were a family. My eyes misted as I thought about leaving in two days. The way he held our daughter and kissed her like he wouldn't see her again cut me deep. I had to make it back here somehow.

CHAPTER 50

GREG

When I dropped them off at the airport, I didn't want to let them go. Her head rested on my chest while our daughter rested in her other arm. I kissed the tops of both of their heads and when Veronica looked up at me, I had to close my eyes. The sadness and the overflow of tears had me wanting to just escort them out of there. She has a signing in a couple weeks that she has to get ready for but she's already stressed to me that she isn't ready to go. I dare say that I've falling in love with a woman that I've shared minimal time with. Our time together is full of deep conversations and laughter, so I feel like I've known her for a lifetime. My sister finally got to meet the baby and as a lawyer, she does not mince words. Her exact words to me were "if mom and dad were here, they'd be pissed that you didn't already have a ring on her finger. Even if she hasn't said it, she loves you." When I catch Veronica staring at me or the way she smiles at me, I can see it. I take her face and kiss her again as her bottom lip wobbles.

"Call me as soon as you get home, okay?"

She nods not trusting her voice. She passes me my daughter and I nuzzle her cheek. Her cold fingers hit my eye and I chuckle. I kiss her knuckles as I remove them from my face and hand her back to her mother. Watching them walk away gut me. She lifted Lyana's hand after they passed through security to wave at me and I of course, waved back. I walked away feeling empty. The car ride home was quiet, the apartment was even more quiet. My keys hitting the counter rang in my ears. When I walked into the bedroom, you could still smell a hint of her perfume. I just sat on the side of the bed and sighed. One day we would make this work but just getting to that one day seemed like an eternity.

Two months have passed since I've seen them in person. I'm sitting in my office staring at one of my favorite pictures. We had walked around the park and Lyana had started to cry. I picked her up and lifted her above my head. Her eyes met mine as I smiled and a line of slobber fell from her mouth as she smiled back. Veronica had snapped the picture and I would forever be grateful that she took it. The picture after this one wasn't as cute though. The slobber had hit my chin and the look of horror on my face was hilarious.

"Greg?"

I turn to the door and see Deena standing there with a smile as she looks at the picture blown up on the wall.

"I love that picture of you two."

"Yeah, me too. What's up?"

"You have a new meeting tomorrow with the Crosby's. They want to purchase space in Veronica's building."

"Oh, good. Okay, thanks."

She smiled and looked at the picture again before leaving. Veronica is in the process of having the building completely renovated for commercial use. She stressed that the whole top floor be reserved for her and her business for when they were in town but the rest of the building can be leased. On top of everything that I have going on in my office with selling, why not take that on as well. The progress on the building was coming along and the designs that she has for a patio on the back were charming. She wanted a space for the buildings tenants so that they would not try to make a move to the roof. She held that space sacred for us and I'm glad that she did. With my phone ringing to release me, I got back to work.

CHAPTER 51

"We're leaving."

Chantel looked up from her computer screen.

"What?"

"Your parents want you close for your father, the building's renovations are just about complete, my contract is up at the end of this month for my gigs and I miss Greg. Lyana is about to turn one, why not move back to the city so that she can grow up like we did? I love the quiet of these mountains but I miss the noise, don't you?"

She stood up and walked over to where I sat with the baby on the floor playing. When she sat next to me, she pulled me into a hug.

"I never wanted to leave you here but I was ready to go back. When mom called me and told me about dad's condition, I knew I needed to be closer to home. I didn't want to hurt your feelings."

"You wouldn't have hurt my feelings. You know I would have followed soon after anyway. When have we been far apart from each other?"

She laughed and the mood lightened.

"I can't wait. I do miss the sounds of the city."

"I've been looking and I found a couple of houses outside the city for a great price. I still want Lyana to have a yard to play in but at least when she comes to work with me, she can see the city."

"Yeah. That would be good. I'll still only be an hour away."

Chantel's parents still owned a house down the street from my parents and they've been helping Chantel's mom with her father. He had just been diagnosed with dementia and her mom has been having a rough time. She didn't want to ask her daughter for help but I knew Chantel would want to be there.

"Yep. Both of our drives will be about a half hour to the office but there isn't a need to be there every day. I can paint anywhere but at least we will have an office if we need it."

"You're so professional."

"Only because of you. This was all your doing. You've kept me balanced and you know that."

"That's what friends are for."

"Right. I'm going to draft up some paperwork for Cunningham. If he wants me to do more shows, he's going to have to fly me here."

"Yes girl! Make them work for you."

We both high-fived and giggled. Looking down at my daughter playing, I know it's the best decision.

∼

CHAPTER 52

VERONICA

he truck has loaded up all of our things as well as my car and will meet us in New York in five days. I take my suitcase and place it in the cab. Chantel has already flown back to the city because her father ended up in the hospital. The doctor's said that they just wanted to keep him for a couple of days and he should be able to go home, which was a relief to hear. I place Lyana into the car seat and join her in the back seat. As the cab pulls away, I look at the house that helped me become who I was. With the market in Nevada being so competitive, my house sold quickly. I was able to close on it last week and the cleaners and painters would be there to get it ready for the new buyers. I smile as I thought about the phone call a couple of months ago to Greg.

"Hello?"

"Hey handsome."

"Hey yourself."

"You wouldn't happen to know who I can call to purchase a house in New York would you?"

The line was quiet. "For whom?" The apprehension in his voice made my stomach flutter.

"For a mom and a daughter. They are looking to move back to the city from the dessert to be closer to her father."

"If this is real, I'll pull up houses today."

I laughed a belly laugh at his eagerness. "It's real. I don't want to live in the city though."

"Veronica, you have no idea how happy this makes me. I'm on it. I'll have some places for you by the end of the day."

"Thank you."

"No. Thank you."

He didn't exaggerate either. There were about ten listings in various suburbs of New York in my email by the end of the day. He told me to mark the ones that I wanted to see and he would go and look at them to make sure everything was good. In the end, I picked a beautiful three-bedroom ranch style home in Kensinton. It was closer to my parents in Philly and about an hour drive to the office. It had a fenced in yard and a two-car garage. Greg being the man that he is, talked the relator down a couple of dollars and I got it for under the asking price. Now, we are flying home so that I can see it with my own two eyes.

The FaceTime with Greg did not do it justice. The house was all refinished inside. The large kitchen flowed into the living and dining room. The large island separated a majority of the space. The wooden floors were a dark grey and the rooms were separated on two sides of the house. My room sat alone on one side and faced a large patio off the back of the house. I also had my own door to leave out of my room to access the outside. Making the move out of the city was the right choice. There were trees that lined the back of the prop-erty which gave lots of privacy. The other two rooms sat behind the kitchen area and the natural light that came from each window was like a breath of fresh air. We would certainly make great memories here. As the baby crawled through the empty house, I walked over and hugged Greg's middle.

"This is absolutely perfect."

"You're perfect."

I couldn't help but to smile. I couldn't wait until my things arrived and I could decorate like I wanted. Until then, we would stay with Greg, which he was excited about.

"HAPPY BIRTHDAY!"

The room erupted in applause as Lyana attempted to blow out her candle. She has just turned two. We stand around the large island in Veronica's house, surrounded by her parents, my sister, Deena, and Chantel. We all wore party hats and Lyana clapped her little hands together as everyone sang. It has been amazing to watch my little girl grow up. Life has really worked out in our favor. Since Veronica has moved back to New York, she's set up her art studio in her building and I've all but moved into the house with her and my daughter. I'm here constantly and we have been enjoying each other's company. Even though we see each other just about every day, we make it a point to meet on the rooftop at midnight every so often. Deena has loved being the honorary babysitter when we meet up. I go back to my apartment when her best friend comes in to visit and love that we have settled into a rhythm so quickly. Things with Veronica and I have gotten serious and I plan to propose this Christmas. She makes me a better person and I love her for it. The building is all but rented out and she has a steady income coming in from the office space occupied. Her art is kept on the top floor which we've added a special key card to access. Her paintings are gaining more traction and now celebrities are buying her work. She has been in high demand as a local black painter. Her rags to riches story resonate with so many people and they want to see her lifted. I'm extremely proud and excited to watch her on this journey. We make eye contact across the island and she smiles. As the cake is passed out and the conversations flow, I grab my drink and walk outside on the patio. Veronica has a small fire going in the firepit already. It's cool but not cold outside so the heat feels good radiating from it. I hear the door open and she steps out to join me.

"Are you okay?" she asks.

"Yeah. I'm just getting some air."

She looks around. "It's nice out here, isn't it?"

"It is." I put my arm around her and pull her close.

"I'm still thinking about the other day."

She's quiet but I can feel her smile against me. I was at my apartment and the baby was with her parents for the weekend. They were to bring her back in time for the party. I had just come from the gym and had gotten out the shower when I received a text.

Meet me at midnight

With life being so busy, we've made time to meet on the rooftop, but never spontaneous like this. I smiled and got dressed. This time, I didn't have to worry about her being there by herself because there were camera's everywhere, except the roof. That space had to remain private and the only way to access it was with a key. I timed my drive perfectly and arrived at just before midnight. As the doors to the elevator opened, I walked through what used to be a hallway. She had transformed the whole floor into an open warehouse space. It looked like an art exhibit. There were easels and art in just about every space. I quickened my pace to the door towards the back and opened it up. The solar lights that were inserted into the floor around the outside lit the space up in a dim but beautiful light. She stood there in a long white flowing dress with a colorful sweater over her shoulders. Her hair was wrapped in her scarf in her signature way. The hair that was visible sat just above her forehead. I placed my hands in my pockets and walked over to her.

"You summoned me?"

Her hands went to my shirt and lay flat against my chest.

"Dance with me."

There was light music playing and I obliged. We swayed and stayed close as the night drew on. She had made the space cozy and there was a chaise that sat against the side of the building so she could lay and watch the stars. She took my hand and led me over. When she turned around, her hands went to her sweater and pushed it from her shoulders. The goosebumps rose on her skin.

"Make love to me?"

She didn't have to ask me twice. I grab the blanket that she uses to cover when its chilly out and place it over her shoulders. As she holds on to it, I take her straps to her dress down and let it pool on the floor. She steps out from the pile and much to my delight, she isn't wearing anything underneath. I sit her down as I disrobe and join her under the blanket. She straddles my hips and as she comes down, she brings the blanket with her. Her heat over top of me as she sets the pace has me closing my eyes. When they reopen, the stars look closer and her face is of pure magic. I have to hold her hips still as I try to regain control. Her smirk tells me that she doesn't want me to. Her body moves with ease over me and I can only watch and enjoy. As she starts to squeeze me, I grip her hips tightly as her chest falls on mine. She cries out and my hips take over for her. Her moans get louder until she sits up and her head falls backwards as her body stiffens. We weren't in a rush, we didn't have a time limit, we were free. This would be by far the best memory from our meetings at midnight.

CHAPTER 54

VERONICA

"Oh my god! Let me see that ring." Chantel excitedly squealed while taking my hand. "Mrs. Veronica Devereux. Sounds so…debonaire. Are you excited?"

I could help but laugh at her excitement. Greg proposed to me on Christmas morning this past year and I was floored. When he went down on one knee in front of the fireplace, my eyes searched out my father who winked at me. He knew and that made the day even more special. I now have a yellow canary diamond on my finger that's worth more than half of the paintings I've sold. I couldn't wait to become his wife. Life with him and Lyana have been like something from a fairy tale. Greg moved out of his apartment and into the house with us because it was like he lived there anyway.

"I'm so excited. I still can't believe this is real. Are you still going with me to my fitting?"

She gave me a chiding look. "You think I would miss that? You know I'll be there."

I have been so nervous about having everything perfect. When the announcement was made in the news, both of our phones have been ringing off the hook. One magazine labeled us old and new money which hurt a little but it comes with the territory, I guess. One good thing that came from this was I found my dress maker rather quickly. A local seamstress approached me and asked me if she could make my dress from scratch. Knowing where I started and knowing how great of a feeling it was when I got that one chance to show what I could do made me say yes. Me and Chantel have met with her multiple times picking out designs. She was so attentive and when my mother found out, she cried. She's always been a sucker for the little guy and this warmed her heart. She promised to help with colors and menus but she wanted to be surprised with the dress. My heart raced with the knowledge that I would be marrying the man who captured my heart on a rooftop. Because of our story, the rooftop is where the wedding will take place. What better way to bring it full circle than to make our commitment in the place we fell in love?

CHAPTER 55

VERONICA

The drive downtown to the seamstress was surprisingly easy. I parked behind the building and waved to Chantel who was sitting in the car parked next to me. She was still living in Philly to help her parents and drove in to be with me this morning. I got out and hugged her before taking her arm and walking into the back door of the shop. The bell dinged above our heads and a petite woman with her hair messily atop her head came around the corner. She had a measuring string around her shoulders, a pencil in her hair and her glasses sat low on her nose. Her smile increased when she saw us standing there.

"Good morning! Come in, come in. I'm finishing up with a walk-in and will be ready in just a minute. There's juice or coffee over there by the fridge."

We thanked her and she whisked around the corner out of view. Me and Chantel started looking at the many half-finished projects she had hanging around and made our way to the front of the store. There was a beautiful woman with long blonde hair standing on a dais as the seamstress measured her waist and stuck push pins into the fabric around her waist. The woman looked to also be getting fitted for a wedding dress. The woman looked over her shoulder towards us and we smiled but she didn't return it. I looked at Chantel who just shrugged. The seamstress looked up and then over to a rack.

"Your dress is right over there. You can take it into the dressing room and try it on if you want. I'm not going to be too much longer here and then we can make any changes you'd want."

"Thank you! I can't wait to see it."

"I can't wait to see it on you." The seamstress smiled.

My eyes made contact to the woman standing. "Are you getting married soon?"

She smirked and looked down her nose at me.

"Yes, soon."

She continued to stare and it made me uneasy so I grabbed my dress and hurried out of the room. When we got to the back, I looked at Chantel in confusion.

"That woman was kind of rude."

"Yeah, and weird."

Chantel took the dress from me and hung it on the hook inside the room.

"Okay, hurry up. I want to see it."

I laughed and curtsied. "Yes ma'am."

After disrobing and unzipping the garment bag, I gasped. The dress was simple and beautiful. The top had so many crystals and dipped low down my cleavage. The bottom was flowing with chiffon. The belt that went around my waist was a dark midnight blue that bowed in the back. I looked like a princess. My dark skin glowed under the lightness of the white fabric and I felt a tear fall down my cheek. I slowly turned around and opened the curtain. Chantel was immediately in tears as she looked at me. Footsteps sounded and we both turned as a figure ran around the corner.

"Wait, stop! You can't go back there!"

The woman that stood on the dais came around the corner

and stopped abruptly. Her face was full of surprise and then she burst into tears. I hurried the tears from my cheeks and started for her but she put her hand out.

"Stop! Don't come any closer."

"Are you okay?" I asked concerned.

"No. No, I'm not. I knew it was you but I had to make sure. How could he leave me for you?"

"Who?"

"You know who! Greg. I was supposed to be marrying him. He was supposed to choose me."

I looked at Chantel for help and she looked angry.

"Who the hell are you, lady?" Chantel asked.

"It doesn't matter anymore."

She closed her eyes and gave me a look that shook me to the core.

"I may just have to come to see if he actually goes along with this sham of a wedding. He knows he'll always belong to me."

"What the…"

She turned and walked out before I could finish. I was so confused and now I'm nervous as hell. *Who in the hell was that?*

"*D*aydreaming again, huh?" Riley says as he stands in the doorway.

I'm sitting in my office and I have a ton of papers that I should be going through but all I can seem to think about is Veronica. I look at all of the pictures that litter my desk of my daughter and smile.

"Can you believe she said yes?"

"To your ass, no!"

We both laugh as Denna comes running into the office. We both look at her as she stops at my desk with a horrified look on her face.

"What is wrong with you?" I ask her.

"Where's your phone?"

I look under a pile of papers and retrieve it. "It's here, why?"

"We have a problem. Jennifer is back."

I look at my phone and don't see any missed calls. "What?"

"Pull up the news."

My chest hurts at the thought of that woman coming back into my life. I still have a restraining order for her so she knows not to come around me. The first article that I pull up has me standing up.

"What the fuck!"

Riley hurries over and looks over my shoulder.

Woman claims to be engaged to real estate guru Gregory Devereux.

There she was, standing with a tissue crying. The article goes on to say that she has been away overseas and she came back to news of another engagement. I could only groan as I pushed Veronica's name and called her.

"Hello?"

"Baby, I need you to come to the office."

"What's wrong? Are you okay?"

"Yes. I'll explain everything when you get here, just please hurry. Are you still downtown?"

"Yes. We just finished up here at the shop."

"Good, good. I'll see you in a minute."

"Okay. I love you."

"I love you too."

I hung up the phone and grabbed my hair. *This can't be happening right now.*

CHAPTER 57

First, the crazy lady at the boutique, now, Greg is acting weird. What the hell is going on?

"Chantel, can you ride with me to Greg's office?"

"Of course."

We were about to go and get lunch after my fitting, but Greg sounded like he was in trouble and I knew I had to hurry. His office was already downtown, so it didn't take long to reach his office. We hurried up the elevator and I smiled at Deena as I walked through the door. Her expression looked pained or sad and I couldn't figure out why. Riley came out of Greg's office as I approached and gave me a hug as I passed. He asked Chantel to go and get coffee with him so that Greg and I could have some privacy. Greg was pacing as I walked in and closed the door.

"Greg? What's wrong?"

He stopped pacing and took a deep breath before handing me his phone. I could feel my brow scrunch as I read the screen and tried to make sense out of what I was seeing. I read the headline and then my heart started beating faster as I looked at the picture. It was the woman from the boutique.

"Greg, who is this? I saw her today."

His face turned pale and he staggered back a little.

"Where? Did she say anything to you? Did she hurt you?"

"Hurt me? Greg… Who is this?"

He closed his eyes and scrubbed his hands down his face as he mumbled to himself. *She was supposed to stay gone. Why is she back?*

"Greg, you're scaring me. Who?"

"Jennifer."

My eyes widened in surprise. He told me about her a while ago during one of our rendezvous on the rooftop.

"What the hell? I thought she moved away."

"So did I. Part of the agreement states that she can't be around me or my family."

"I guess I'm not family yet so I'm fair game."

"Dammit. Had I known that she would resurface, I wouldn't have allowed the announcement to go out."

"This isn't your fault. Should I worry about Lyana?"

"No. If she went anywhere near her, I wouldn't wait for the police to show up."

I had never seen Greg this upset before and I knew that this was serious.

"What should we do?"

"Let me call my sister and see what she says. As of now, just be careful. I would feel better knowing that you're working from your building where there's cameras."

"I can do that."

"And, if people aren't invited, they will not know of where we are getting married. I'm glad that I left that out of the announcement."

"Me too." I stand up and smile at him as I walk his phone back to him. "What a way to start off our lives, huh?"

"I won't let anything happen to you."

I stand on my tiptoes and kiss him. "I know."

He hugs me tight and kissed my forehead as the door opens

and Riley and Chantel come through the door. Riley's hand swiftly leaves Chantels lower back and I look at Greg to see if he saw too.

"Riley filled me in. I've already called my mom; I'm staying in the city until they get this figured out."

"She can stay with me." Riley joins in.

I give Chantel a look and she looks away. *Riley and Chantel? What happened to Kita?* I smirk and I could feel Greg chuckle as my head stays on his chest.

CHAPTER 58

GREG

It was almost a week until we found out where Jennifer was staying. Her mother felt sorry for her living in the Midwest and invited her to stay with her after reading about the wedding in the news. She thought that she may not be able to handle the news by herself. My sister got Veronica's name added to the restraining order to make sure she was covered. Jennifer's mom didn't even know that she had made contact. She told her mother that she couldn't take seeing me happy in the news so she was going back to her home in Kansas. Now, we know that to be a lie. She'd been staying in a shelter on the outskirts of town and we only found that out by looking at the many street-cam videos to track her whereabouts. The police escorted her back to her mother's house and told her to make sure she makes it back to Kansas. If she comes back to New York, she will be arrested and placed in custody of the state. We never wanted the public to know about her mental health issues and kept everything private but with this latest development, we couldn't leave it to chance. Veronica means the world to me and I would not have this overshadow our wedding. None of this was her fault and I felt bad that she canceled her bridal shower in fear of Jennifer wrecking anything. We have exactly three months before I marry the woman of my dreams and I won't let anything or anyone come between that.

CHAPTER 59
VERONICA

"Girl, are you sure that crazy lady won't show up to the wedding?" Chantel asked as we ate our dinner.

I was getting married in two weeks and she drove up from Philly to help finalize everything. Greg and I just signed our marriage certificate while Chantel and Riley witnessed. It was finally coming together and we needed some girl time before things got hectic. Lyana chose that moment to reach onto my plate and take my fries.

"Hey!" I exclaimed as Lyana laughed. I shook my head and gave her a pinched look. I looked back over to Chantel who was smiling at us. "I'm not worried. Greg said that she's gone and I trust him."

"I swear, if that chick shows up, I might just trip her over the side of the building."

"Chantel!"

She looks at the baby and laughs. "She's two, she doesn't understand."

"Yeah, tell that to the daycare. She's said 'fuck' every day this week. It's a good thing that the daycare is in the building I own or she would have been put out."

Chantel starts to speak in a smaller voice. "Nobody's gonna put my baby out of daycare."

Lyana blew her godmother a kiss and I rolled my eyes. *These two are doing too much.* I've tried to talk to Chantel about what was happening between her and Riley but both have been tight lipped about it all. She's never been one to hold a secret but me and Greg know that something happened between them. They've both been acting weird.

CHAPTER 60

GREG

The day of the wedding is here and I'm nervous as hell. I hadn't seen Veronica in two days and I missed her already. She took the baby and went to stay with her mother until the wedding. As Riley and I approached the building, I looked up at its many floors from the outside and smiled. This is the place that changed my life. Not only was it my first building, but it was also the place where I fell in love. Riley clapped me on the back.

"Are you ready?"

"Yes, very much so."

He smiled and placed a hand on my back as I walked into the building. There were bright floor lights that led to the elevator and I was taken back to the first night we met on the rooftop. Our steps echoed as we approached the elevator and everything was in slow motion. I could feel my heart racing as the doors opened and we stepped inside. With each floor that we rose, I could feel the adrenaline pumping in my veins. When we reached the top, I looked over at my best friend and smiled. He's been with me through it all and I couldn't do this without him. We walked down the hall past all of her art and out the door to the roof. The sun was still high in the sky and it was moving slowly across the sky to set soon. My sister stood up front talking to someone and when her eyes caught mine, I saw the tears well in her eyes. Our parents would be proud to see us both now. She excused herself and came into my arms for a hug.

"You look so good big brother."

I smiled against her cheek. "Thanks. You look like mom."

I felt her nod against me because she knew it. After we let each other go, I kissed her cheek and shook hands with the woman officiating the wedding. This woman has been friends with Veronica's family since Veronica was a child and she insisted that she officiate as a wedding present to us both. Veronica was overjoyed and to see her happy makes me happy. We didn't have to wait long because as soon as I shook the last hand, someone announced that the limo had arrived. I looked over at Riley and my cheeks hurt from smiling so hard.

"Here we go."

$\mathcal{M}$y mother and father looked so beautiful. My mom had on a beautiful navy dress with silver shoes and my father's tie matched her perfectly. Chantel was in tears the whole way to the venue and I could only chuckle. She had been my rock and seeing her cry made my lump grow bigger in my throat. She held a sleeping Lyana in her lap and gently pat her back. When the limo turned the corner and the building came into view, it all became so real. The driver parked and came to open the back doors. My father got out first and helped my mother to stand. She put her arms out and took Lyana who had just woken up. My father helped Chantel out next and placed his hand down for mine. My hand shook as I placed it in his and he squeezed.

"I got you, baby girl."

I didn't trust my voice and I could only smile. My mother walked ahead of us and someone opened the door. The lights on the floor made me bark a laugh. They all looked at me and I shook my head because they wouldn't understand the significance. My mother thought the lights were a nice touch but I knew the meaning behind them. We rode the elevator up and I could only look at the people who made me who I was. My mother and father laughed and whispered in each other's ears and it was so cute and innocent. Lyana had her head laid on my mother's shoulder while Chantel pushed a stray hair from Lyana's forehead. The doors opened and I took my father's arm. Chantel stopped in the middle of the hall and turned to me.

"Ready?"

I nodded my head and she smiled a huge smile before walking out the door. The music started playing and my stomach clenched. Mom put Lyana on the floor and took her hand. As the door opened, Lyana must have seen her father.

"Daddy!"

I heard the crowd giggling and then overshadowed by awes. My mother looked back at me and winked before the door closed and I stood there alone with my dad.

"Thank you, daddy."

"For what?"

"Teaching me what to look for in a man."

His breath caught and he didn't have time to answer as the music changed and we started forward. The door opened and we stepped out into the setting sun. There was a haze over the other buildings and a soft breeze was blowing. I looked up at my dad who had a tear rolling down his cheek and I wanted to wipe it away. I gripped his arm tighter and he pat my hand in understanding.

"Mommy!"

I looked at my perfect little girl in the arms of the man I loved. The man that I almost didn't have. To think that I didn't tell him about her for so long and now here we are getting married. I looked up into Greg's eyes and he had tears welled that hadn't fell yet. He mouthed the word beautiful and I looked down. When his feet came into view, my father turned me and lifted my veil and kissed my cheek and placed my veil back over my face. I closed my eyes as I seen my father cry and he pulled me into a hug. When he let go, he shook Greg's hand and then placed my hand into Greg's. He put his arms out and Lyana went willingly into his arms as he went to sit next to my mom. I handed my flowers to Chantel who stood beside me and turned back to Greg. Looking into his eyes, I saw how much he loved me. Standing here on this rooftop with him brought back every laugh, every cry, every dream. This place was ours and will forever be. Our hearts were laid bare on this rooftop and today, we would solidify our feeling in front of all the ones we love.

CHAPTER 62

GREG

*S*he's mine. The words were spoken, the kiss was sealed, the drinks were poured and the music was played. It's just us now. Everyone laughed and congratulated us and then as the night wore on, they left. Now, here we are, just the two of us dancing on the rooftop. My watch sounds and I smile down at my wife.

"It's midnight."

She looks up at the stars and smiles. "Yep, it's midnight."

From nothing to something, from something to nothing. We've seen it all and we've seen it together. Who knew that love at first sight existed? Our story isn't like most but it's ours. If she would have never answered that note to meet me at midnight, this could have ended before it even started. She's mine and I'll never let her go.

"Did you have a good time?" She asks.

I'm broke out of my thoughts as she speaks. "Hm? Yeah, I did."

"Good, because your life is about to change."

"Oh yeah? How are you going to do that?"

"Well, you missed everything with the first so now you get a second chance."

I was confused. "Our second chance?"

"No. YOUR second chance. With this baby."

I gasp and held her away from me. "What? A baby?"

"Yep. Just found out last week."

"Does anyone know?"

She shook her head. "Just you. I needed you to be the first to know. Things didn't go as planned with the first so now this time we do it together."

I take her face in my hands and kiss her deep. "I love you, Mrs. Devereux."

"I love you too, Mr. Devereux."

I think I'll correct my former statement. THIS will be my favorite meeting at midnight.